BURTON WITH THE THOUSAND

BURTON WITH THE THOUSAND
Being the Second Adventure of Burton the Red

by

Sandro Dariosto

per sempre Anita Edizione
Ferrara Seattle
2014

Printed in the United States of America

per sempre Anita Edizione
via delle Scienze 17 Ferrara

10 9 8 7 6 5 4 3 2 1

To the happy few

. . . destiny prefers to repeat forms, and what happened once happens often.

--Jorge Luis Borges

Burton with the Thousand
or,
How Il Rosso Lost His Heart Forever

I.

I was returning to my office at the University of M_____ when my brother's telegram arrived. He'd sent it to me there, not knowing if I could be reached in the little one room, basement flat where I lived on a grad student stipend. Rita, the Department secretary, was waiting for me with it, the yellow envelope still in her hand, because she knew it had to be important if it came in a telegram. And of course, it was killing her not to be able to open it.

So I tore it open in front of her, not letting her see, and it read simply this:

"Come quick. Siracusa. Albergo Domus Mariae. I have found him. R."

The wire had been sent from Augusta, Sicily, that very morning. I took it upstairs to the corner of the old Granmora where my desk sat in a room with five other desks that belonged to the five other Teaching Assistants, and I sat down and read it a couple of times over, as if those ten words on the yellow paper might grow into more if I stared at them long enough. But I didn't really need any more, and my brother knew that. He had found him. After fifteen years or more, I added it up in my head. Rob had found him. He didn't even need to say who it was, for I knew: it was Il Rosso.

After a quick trip to the library, I figured out where exactly in the world Augusta was. And then over that night with a lot of prayerful arithmetic and the hope of an advance, as I maxed out my first credit card, I began to find a way. When the morning came, I went out and bought a plane ticket to Catania, both ways, to cover my spring break. Those two weeks of holiday would have to be enough, because I had no more time, and if the truth be told, I didn't have the time or the resources to do even what I did.

I sent Rob a return telegraph that said only: "Siracusa. March 19." Pinching my pennies with every word, I didn't even sign it.

While I'd been in college and then graduate school, my brother had dropped out, done a quick turn in the post-Vietnam Army, and learned to fly a helicopter. He worked now all around the world as a helicopter pilot, but mostly at construction sites in what they call "developing" countries. We kept in touch, but in only intermittent ways.

The last I'd heard from him had been at Christmas time, when he'd shipped me a bottle of Marsala and a three foot tall Sicilian puppet from Gela. He was flying for some corporation with a vague European name I didn't recognize, building offshore oil derricks in the Mediterranean. The puppet, with its pitch black mustache and coffee brown face, all dressed in tin armor with a sword in one hand, was a crusader Rob said. But I think, by the look of that puppet's face, that he hadn't sent me any crusader, whatever Rob thought. He was a Saracen. I wrote him a letter to tell him as much, and sent it with a bottle of Kentucky bourbon to his address in Gela. But I never heard if he received it.

So that was it. We'd not spoken or written since, until the telegram arrived.

*   *   *

My plan was to grade papers on the long flight from Chicago to Milan and then on to Catania, but somehow that didn't happen. Instead my mind wandered through the adventures that Il Rosso had spun about his time in the Anzani Legion, riding and fighting with the Garibaldini across the north of Italy. All the tales he'd told us in his tent, those nights fifteen years ago, how those tales had grown over time in our minds and how he'd enchanted us, my little brother and me. Then there was the way he'd disappeared into the night in his long, red Buick convertible, with its white canvas top, pulling a trailer that was supposed to be filled with Zambutti Sam, the wild mountain gorilla. How he had enchanted us, indeed, and how we still talked about him and searched for him.

You see, Il Rosso was maybe the reason for my brother's wanderlust, for everywhere on the planet that Rob landed, he asked after and searched for traces of that man. And my brother had found work that let him wander the world in search. And whenever we spoke, Rob and I, Il Rosso was always just beneath the surface. Rob would say, "I'm headed to Argentina next spring." He didn't have to say, 'Maybe I'll find some sign of him there.' It was understood.

Now and then, he would write or call to say that he'd run into someone who recognized that name, Jack Burton, or who remembered a guy in a wheelchair and a red shirt, or had been to a little circus with a trained mountain gorilla.

3

And then Jack Burton would come up directly. But Rob never found more than such small hints, and always before his search had led to nowhere.

Until now. And on my Alitalia flight I was restless, because the words on that telegram kept appearing before my eyes. "I have found him," it read. Il Rosso. Found.

And so the long flights passed with a lot of little bottles of red wine and crystal clear grappa, and no papers graded, and too much staring out the window at the tops of gray Atlantic clouds, or black night sky, and at dawn the snowy peaks of the Alps.

As I waited in Milan for the connecting flight to Catania, I tried to read about Siracusa from a guidebook I'd checked out of the library, but nothing would stick in my mind. The words just lay flat on the page and I couldn't connect more than one or two at a time, and always they led straight back to my wandering thoughts of Il Rosso. "I have found him."

It was a short train ride from Catania to Siracusa, and along the way we passed Augusta: just an ugly industrial port, all tanker ships and pipelines. At Siracusa Stazione, I took a cab to the hotel. It rattled through the littered and tired streets of that sad, worn downtown, coated with Sicilian dust and grime. But then we crossed the bridge on Corso Umberto and suddenly everything changed. It was dusk as we wound past the remains of some ancient temple, and then dove into the narrow, shadowy medieval streets of Ortigia. For a moment I thought I was being had, taken on the wild ride of the American tourist. I began to count the little change in my pockets, wondering how much the driver would take me for, cursing my brother and his wild wandering ways, under my breath. For just a moment, I longed for the security of my basement apartment and my stacks of student papers to read. But for only a moment.

Then, before I could mutter anymore, the little Fiat cab jerked out of the dark and crooked street onto a corso that opened out along the Ionian Sea. The driver pulled up in front of a three storey stone building, turned back to me and announced, "Domus Mariae." The face of the old building had a bright white light casting up into the Sicilian dusk off the old stones. I crawled out of the cab, paid the driver a true pittance, took my bag and, with a cough and a sputter, the little Fiat was gone.

At my back, across the tiny street, stood a church, its spires lit indirectly by the bright light of the albergo. I had to buzz to have the wrought iron gate to the hotel opened. Then it was up a narrow stone stairs, well lit, spotlessly clean, to the second floor where, to my surprise, I was greeted in Sicilian by a nun.

"'Sera, Sorella," I said, hesitatingly, and then told her my name.

She took up English immediately, and welcomed me to the Convent of St. Ursula.

"Convent?" I said.

She just smiled, then she went behind her desk and pulled out a big iron key and a square, white envelope.

The Sorella was actually quite young and pretty, I noticed even in her drab black habit. She said, "Follow me; you are already registered." And then she led me up to my room. "Your fratello wanted this room for you," she said, as she opened the door, and led me into the dark.

Instead of turning on the lights, she slipped across the room and threw open two shutters that ran from floor to the high ceiling, and into the dark room charged the soft evening lights of Ortigia glancing off the Ionian Sea below. The gentle roar of the waves spoke in the silence.

It was in that reflected, starry light I saw the twin beds against the opposite wall, and as the pretty Sorella turned to leave, I asked, "Is he here?"

"Your fratello will be back tomorrow," she said. "He left you this." And then she handed me the envelope in her hand, along with the big iron key to the room.

"Breakfast begins at 6 in the morning," she said, "If you like, " and then with a "buona sera," she left.

The evening light outside was too delicate; a lamp would destroy it. So I stepped out through the dark wood shutter onto the balcony and opened Rob's envelope in the starlight and the sea shine. There were two pages inside, and the first was Rob's scrawl across a piece of Domus Mariae stationary.

"Back Tuesday," his note read. "The job is done this weekend, then I'm free. So settle in and I'll be there soon. Kaliope is a good trattoria, if you're hungry. A presto, Rob"

Then he added this post script: "Read this and you'll see what I mean."

The other paper inside the envelope was a yellowed sheet, folded in half, brown and brittle at the fold. I opened it gently, trying not to break it. But then a sweet evening breeze drifted up from the sea, and ruffled the papers in my hand. So I stepped back inside the room, sat on one of the beds and resignedly switched on the lamp.

In the yellow light I scanned that old piece of paper and saw first that it was all in Italian. So I didn't try to read it, but my eyes dropped to the bottom of the page and I saw the signature. "Burtoni," it read in a bold black scrawl.

Was this Jack Burton? This bold scribble? This "Burtoni"? How could Rob be so sure? Were we just on some wild pursuit again? Was I spending all my time and every cent I had and more for my little brother's latest pipe dream of finding Il Rosso? "Burtoni" it said in a heavy hand. The name Jack Burton called himself, when he told us his story beside that circus tent, while the sweet strange smoke of his pipe filled the air, more intoxicating than his words.

But I was red-eyed and so jet lagged I couldn't tell you what time of day it was, and I knew that making out the Italian on that old slip of paper was beyond me, just then. Still I knew enough to realize the worst thing I could do was to sleep, and thus stay forever in the jet lagged world of lost time.

So I folded the letter up again carefully, put it in my jacket pocket and unpacked enough to find my dictionary. The pretty little Sorella gave me directions to Kaliope, and I wandered out into the ancient streets of Ortigia, to find something to eat.

Rob was right about the trattoria. Kaliope served me misto fritto of local seafood for antipasto and a breaded cutlet Palermitana for the secondi, all of it washed down by a mezzo of the house wine, served in a short ceramic pitcher. And they played a wonderful brand of old Italian jazz, Gorni Kramer's blues accordion and Renato Selani's piano, that went with the wine and made me feel right at home. Ugo, the owner, who of course knew my brother, brought over a bittersweet liqueur, flavored with almonds, after I was done. "'Berto always has this," he said. Then realizing he was talking to Rob's brother, he pronounced my brother's name with a flat, American accent that rattled from his tongue with difficulty. "Raaab always drinks one of these," and then he added, "We make it ourselves."

And so, warmed by the wine and then by that sweet liqueur, I took out "Burtoni's" letter and began, with my dictionary and some help from Ugo, and a gentleman named Marcello at the table next to me, to translate it. "Mia Rafaela Carissima" it began:

My Dearest Rafaela,
What can I say to you, at this point? How can I make you see? I could say I didn't know, but it is true, I did. The firing squad was my duty. There were orders from the General himself. And you know, it was me he sent because it was me he trusted. Because it was I he knew.

He did not know Lombardo. He knew only of the revolt at Castellnotte, and that these sorts of massacres could not be allowed. Not by our side, not by our partisans. And so the orders came from Colonel Bixio, endorsed by the General himself. Giovanni and I went out to set things in order.

So Rosalino is dead now. And almost all of us who were with him. Only you and I and Giovanni now can tell the true story of that journey across the Nebrodi.

I want only some word from you, that you understand. Forgiveness is too big a word. I do not

*ask for forgiveness. If you read this, you will see. It
is the work of Giovanni Corrao, not mine. I ask you
only to understand, and to know that
You will live in my heart forever,
Your Burtoni*

After I'd made the letter out, and finished with Ugo's liquor, I wandered the streets of Ortigia, wondering as I strolled how Rob could be so sure that this old undated letter in Italian could be the trace of Jack Burton he was searching for. The spring evening was cool, and in the stone streets a scattering of people strolled hither and thither, in no hurry. Beside the Fontana Archimedea I paused at a café for another bitter to finish the night and tried out my schoolbook Italian on the locals.

We talked about the marzipan in rows of bowls in the café window, little painted tomatoes and cherries and limes and bananas, tiny but so true to life.

"Mia Madre makes them here," the barista told me, "in the back there." He pointed to a closed door.

The hesitant conversation reminded me of how poor my Italian was, and of how both Rob and I had taken it up in school, because of those long ago nights in that circus tent when Jack Burton had salted his yarn with the exclamations and expressions of Risorgimento Italian. Later, when I'd learned a bit of the language, I realized that Burton always spoke with the rhythm and the music of his adopted language, his English was filled with the music of Italian. And this, these sounds, made his words light up and soar in our ears. It was part of the magic of listening to him, part of his enchantment.

The fountain was lit from below, and the shooting spires of water sparkled in the light. It was all so enticing here: the food, the wine, the tumbling waters, the sparkling light. Yet I couldn't help but think that maybe it was all marzipan, just painted sugar, too sweet to eat, but beautiful to look at, though seeming always real and substantial, seeming the fruit of the vineyards and orchards of this hard land. But really it was just a liquor so sweet it made your eyes swim with pleasure, and strong enough to dim your vision for hours at a time.

How could Rob know this old letter had anything at all to do with our old Il Rosso? How did he come upon it? Why was he so certain of what he had?

I wandered back to the Domus Mariae, more than a little drunk, I suppose, more than a little lost, I'm sure, filled with dreams of Il Rosso. But more than filled with doubts.

In the morning the pretty little nun from the night before was gone, replaced by a sallow young man called Ciccio with bad teeth, a smoky voice and no English. I had cappuccino in the café downstairs and pulled out the old letter to read it again without the help of wine and liquor and jet lag. It made no more sense than it did before, and that made me even more uncertain of my brother and his whims. But I looked out on the smooth face of the Ionian Sea, with its long gray oil tankers drifting across the horizon like mirages in the distance, and reminded myself that Aeschylus and Plato had walked these very stone streets. Cicero had loved this very same view. Whatever Rob was up to, this was a place with its beauty worn deep into its stones for thousands of years, and it was a place now, for me, to simply enjoy. The pastry was sweet and fresh, the coffee was too good to believe. The oranges were a deep and godlike red. Soon 'd see my brother, and this would be a spring break with a good story to tell. No matter what it meant.

I went to the morning market by the Ponte Umbertino and bought cheese and fruit and a bottle of wine, and then I found a place by the Fonte Aetusa to sit and eat and gaze at the sea, while the swans and ducks glided across the tiny, soiled pond they called a fountain. When I strolled back to the hotel in the early afternoon, Ciccio was gone and the little Sorella was back, even more pretty than before. When I asked for the key, she smiled brightly and said my brother had it. Upstairs.

I admit it was with a turn and a running step that I bolted up the stairs, and I banged my forehead on the low corner ceiling. But it didn't stop me. When I turned the knob it was unlocked and so I burst in and found my brother, with his back to me, sitting in a straight backed wooden chair, his legs splayed out wide, his feet in boots firmly planted. From behind, his shoulders were broad and flat under a red t-shirt, and I could see where he was balding at the crown of his head. But his head was almost shaved, so it was only the absence of black stubble that showed his early balding.

He looked up from what he was reading, and I saw the same black stubble on his chin, surrounding his grin. He shouted my name out, and then he was on his feet, he set the book on the chair, and we were hugging hard in the center of the room.

It had been three years now since our father died, leaving Rob and me alone in the world it seemed. Mother has been gone a dozen years or more, gone to a throat cancer that spread fast and took her, and left my Father bereft with a loss from which he would never recover. By the time Dad died in a sudden car accident, I guess it seemed a relief, an end to his ongoing grief. Rob and I were both, then, out and on our own, chasing these wildly different lives of ours. But suddenly we were all the family we had. Two brothers, alone in the world and unattached. It made us closer than we might have been, had our parents lived long and well into a happy old age. I suppose it made this strange search for Jack Burton more vivid, too, in its own way. This search for Il Rosso was the only real point of contact we had now, our lives had become so separate. And so I guess we clung to it.

What followed were the 'how the hell are you's' and the 'you're looking old's' that you'd expect. Lots of thumping on shoulders and slapping on knees, and of course there was a wine bottle opened.

Still it didn't take long before I asked him what it was he was reading. It sat there on his chair still, by the balcony, an old leather bound book, worn and frayed at the edges. On the floor beside the chair lay a couple of leather laces, as old as the book. I reached down to pick it up but Rob warned me off.

"Careful," he said. "It's falling apart."

"What is it?"

"It's Jack Burton's journal," Rob said, and then he took a drink from his wine glass. "The diary of Il Rosso, when he rode with the Thousand across this island. With Garibaldi and the Thousand."

I cracked it open. "Are you sure?" I said and saw the same bold scrawl running across the pages, unnumbered and loose now from their old binding.

"I think so," Rob nodded thoughtfully. Then he reached over and took it from me, closing it carefully and then picking the laces off the floor, he gently bound the old leather volume back together. "I think it is," he repeated, as if to convince himself.

"Where did it come from?" I asked.

Rob didn't answer me, he just tucked the volume carefully in his pack.

"And the letter?" I said, pulling it out of my coat pocket. "Where did you find this?" I said.

Rob reached for it, but with a grin I pulled it away and tucked it carefully in my pocket again. He laughed. "Let's get something to eat," he said. "I'm too hungry. Then I'll tell you all about it, over dinner."

"With the thousand!" I said, as we headed off across the Corso Matteotti, just coming to life for the evening passeggiata. "I Mille. But that's better than a hundred and twenty years ago."

"You're the history major," Rob said, striding ahead of me on the Corso.

"But that means he was over 100 back when we knew him, at home," I said.

"That's old news," Rob said, as he stepped in the door of a café on the edge of Piazza Archimedea. "You've already said that. Many times, Will. Too many times."

Then he ordered us both espresso and ignored me while he spoke easy Italian with the barista. I found myself eyeing the marzipan again. "Show off," I said.

"When in Siracusa," he said in Italian, "speak with the Siragusans." And I noticed then he pronounced the "c"

13

in the city's name with the clipped and guttural "g" of the Sicilians.

After an hour of strolling around, Rob still had not answered any of my questions. He bought us each a cannolo at a café for later, and found a little tourist store where he bought a jar of red marmalade, and handled a little crusader puppet like the one he'd sent me for Christmas. Before long the doors of the restaurants were opening, and he led us around near the Piazza del Duomo to the side street where Trattoria Kaliope lay.

Ugo greeted us with excitement and he sat us at a table next to the kitchen so he could linger and chat, when the business permitted. We never ordered. The food that Ugo chose for us just came in waves. Over a full pitcher of the house wine, Rob told us his story.

"Just like I always do, when I landed at the terminal in Augusta, I started asking around. Taormina and the touristy spots north didn't seem like the kind of places worth looking in. Catania seemed too big, too easy to get lost in, so I headed south on the trains. I'd just get off at one town or another, find a local hang out, ask around if anybody had seen or heard of Jack Burton. Or of Il Rosso, or Gianni Burtoni.

"Who knows what he was calling himself, but I knew that if he'd been around, he'd be remembered. So it was like always. The train station in Lentini, an evening in Belvedere at a café, a bar in Grammiche. I tried little towns, and into the interior, but no trace. Catania was still there waiting, but it seemed impossible to grab a hold of, and maybe not where Jack Burton would spend much time anyway.

"Still, everywhere I went I struck out. Not a sign of him. But you know, I'm used to that. It's the way it always goes. And it's sort of my little entertainment. A way to get out and meet people, you know. Hang with the locals. I was going to be here in Augusta for six to nine months. There was plenty of time to wander about.

"So one weekend, about a month ago, I wandered in here because a guy in a café down by the Ponte said the fish was good.

"After a glass of wine and a little swordfish involtini, I started asking around, and Ugo here, he started to laugh.

"See, he remembered an old Americano, when he was a boy, who came into his father's restaurant, spoke great Italian, and was looking for anybody named Crisianna. Ugo remembered him, because he was in a wheelchair."

"It's true," Ugo interrupted us, speaking in Italian. "He was named Burtoni, and he said he'd lived around here once, long, long ago. But all this happened when I was just a little ragazzo, and we didn't see many Americans then. And even if we did, he was different. So I remembered him."

"Crisianna," I said. "Who was that?"

"You'll see, you'll see," Rob held up his hand. But then someone came in the door of Kaliope, and Ugo was gone to seat them, and another waiter arrived with two pork cutlets, breaded in the Sicilian way.

"So how do we know this Burtoni of Ugo's was our Jack Burton?" I said.

But Rob was deep into the pleasure of his plate, he held up a piece of cutlet on his fork and said, "You like it?" and then set into chewing it.

When Ugo sauntered back, a few moments later, keeping an eye on the door and the kitchen, both, the story went on.

15

"Signor Burtoni could maneuver around in that wheelchair like he was driving a Ferrari, my friends. That's what really impressed me, the way he could handle that thing. Made me want one of my own. A wheelchair! Mio Dio! But my Papa told him, 'Yes, little Sister Crisianna, she is at the convent.'"

"Who is this 'Crisianna'?" I said.

"That's just what your brother kept saying," Ugo laughed.

"But then Ugo tells me this nun was still here," Rob said, his hand holding the fork and gesturing now at the air. "She's running a hotel for the order."

"The Domus Mariae," I said.

Rob nodded, "Suor Crisianna," he said.

"Not that cute little sorella at the desk?"

Ugo laughed at that.

"No, of course not," Rob said. Then he grinned at me, "So you noticed her too."

Ugo liked that even better, but he put on a phony wooden face and crossed himself "Sister Crisianna is as old and tough as the stones of Siracusa," he said in Italian.

"So, to make a long story short, I go off and find this nun who runs the albergo and Ugo is right. She's a tough one. Not a smile or a blink when I ask her about Il Rosso. Nothing."

"He tells her that I sent him," Ugo said, placing a palm on his chest. Then he let the hand course through the air like he was chasing off a butterfly. He rolled his eyes back dramatically, "that didn't help," he said.

Rob chuckled and went on, "I stayed at the albergo, so I could go back three times to see her. The first time to ask her about him, and that time I described Il Rosso. Nothing. The second time I told the sister about you and me, two kids, and how we found him with the circus, way

16

off in America. How we fell in love with him. How we wanted to run away with him. Still, nothing. Not a word about him. About anything, really."

Ugo wiped his palm straight down over his face. "La Suor di Pietra," he said, "the Sister of Stone."

"So I gave up, but one last time as I was checking out of the Domus, I asked after her. She was back in the office, hidden away, scowling at the books. I pressed my way in anyway and I thanked her for the pleasant stay, and for all her time, for listening to me.

"That was when she pulled this out," he patted the bag beside him on the floor where he had the notebook tucked away. "She had it under her desk and suddenly she handed it over to me. And she handled it like it was a holy missal or something.

"'This may be what you're looking for,' she said. If I hadn't come back that last time, really the fourth time I'd bothered her, she'd never have given it to me.

"I didn't ask her what it was. She didn't say anything to me about bringing it back. She knew once I'd read it, she would see me again. I just took it, whatever it was, and rode the train back up to Augusta. At night after work I'd read it, and after a couple of days, I wired you."

"What makes you think it is his," I said.

Ugo leaned over and chuckled right at me. "You're no romantic, Signore, like your brother," he said. But then someone else appeared in the doorway of the trattoria and Ugo had to go back to work.

"You read it over, tonight. Then you can tell me you don't think it's him," Rob answered.

"Is it in Italian? Like the letter? Because, brother, I'm too tired to try to read it in Italian tonight." What I meant was the wine had been too good at dinner for me to attempt to read anything in Italian.

Rob just shook his head no. "It's English. But the letter, in Italian, it was stuck in the back of the book. I'm not sure what to make of that."

"What do you mean?"

"You'll see," was all he'd say.

As we strolled slowly back to the hotel, Rob stopped at the café where he'd bought our cannoli, and he ordered me a double shot of coffee. He had another glass of wine and he broke out our desert at a table in the square. Then he handed me the old notebook across a little café table, and said, "Read it, brother. Read enough of it to convince yourself."

So Rob sipped at his wine and made occasional small talk with passers by, and with the barista, when he went back inside for more wine. The Piazza Archimedea was busy that time of night, even though only this little bar and another café were still open. Still the people of Ortigia we're strolling and talking away as the night air grew slowly cooler.

The leather on the notebook was old and frayed, and the binding was broken so some pages were loose and floating free. Inside the front cover, embossed in the leather, was the name of the binder. 'Liguria Libri,' it said. And then underneath, 'Genova.' There was no mention of Italia, since at the time this book was bound, Italia was only a wild-eyed dream, a seditious idea burning in a few rebellious minds.

Nowhere could I find any place where the writer who had filled this book with words had written his name. The book was inscribed nowhere and to no one. But the handwriting I recognized immediately. It belonged to the same "Burtoni" who had written the letter I had in my pocket. I was full of good food and wine, but the jolt of coffee and then the yarn told in the old pages kept me awake. Here follows a fair copy of what I could make out in the journal of Jack Burton, called herein Burtoni, but known by us all as Il Rosso.

1.

27 March 1860

We are two days out at sea as I finally start to write this down. I meant to begin right from the moment it all commenced, to keep a true record of this adventure for all of time just as it happened, for if we succeed, as I trust we will, we will change the course of history for the rest of the ages. So was my intention, but our departure at night from the port of Genova in secret was greeted first by pursuit from the old blue navy of Savoy, and then by the rush of hard weather that nearly swamped us. These are not good omens for the future of our voyage, but we know, all of us, that omens can be damned. It is the time. It has come. We must press on.

As Count Pilo has said, many times in the last 48 hours, "This time, comrades, we will make Italy or we will die."

We are only three, and I will tell you about each of us, from what I know, later on, when there is time. But tonight as the half moon rests on the quiet sea at last, let me say that we are all of us patriots, republicans deep in our hearts. And all of us have fought beside the General, or been sent into exile with Mazzini. And we go now together to begin the revolution.

Two nights ago, after midnight, we embarked without a light aboard. But no more had we slipped away from the peaceful Genova harbor in our little twelve-foot paranza, rowing quietly out to sea, when the Savoy patrol saw us.

"We've been spotted," Corrao whispered out from the starboard where he held his oar.

"Pull hard, men," cried Pilo. "For Italia."

And so, as Corrao and I worked the oars in unison, our commander Rosalino Pilo left the tiller and lifted the two sails to the breeze.

I saw a series of lanterns blink and flash across the black water and I knew that the shore patrol was signaling to someone between us and the open sea. In the cloudy night, the ocean breeze blew in toward land, and it took Pilo a good long while to get our lateen sails up and the paranza turned right to feel the wind. And in that time, from behind me, a long schooner drifted into sight, its rows of lights brighter than the scattered lights of midnight Genova. Suddenly she was in pursuit of us.

"Pull harder, boys," Pilo cried out, because we were not secret anymore.

The black schooner was bearing down on us, having the advantage of the wind behind her. The lanterns shone out on the dark water, and the schooner cut closer to us and we could hear clearly their calls for us to pull up and to identify ourselves.

I'm sure that many aboard that royal schooner would be on our side, if they knew where we were sailing. I'm certain that on her decks stood seamen who would choose to join us in our cause. But we all knew, Pilo, Corrao and I, that if they stopped us, all would be lost. For officially, the governments of the North are sworn to treaties and truces, and the raising of rebellions is not in their plans. Not in their open and public plans, at any rate. Whatever the sailors on that black schooner believed, her Captain would arrest us, he would seize our little boat and its meager cargo, and then he would turn us all over to the military police in Genova. We will be hung or sent back into exile. They can not do otherwise. We knew this rebellion will end before it even starts, if we are stopped.

The schooner fired a warning shot, to halt us, a single cannon fired over our bow to announce their firm command of the situation. The shot plunged out into the sea ahead of us, and rocked our little boat.

"Pull, boys," cried the Count through his clenched teeth, as he fought with the tiller to bring our ship around and use the wind to make a run close along the coast. In the dark, and close in, there was a chance for us to make our escape, where the schooner could not follow.

In our shallow hold we have only a couple week's food and a few dozen old muskets, with enough ammunition and some fine bayonets to make them presentable, and one crate of grenades. Not much to start a revolution, but all we had. And the Captain of that schooner doesn't know that this is all we carry. He is in pursuit of smugglers, running contraband tobacco and brandy. We are thieves running in the darkest of the night. For him, it is just a evening patrol, the routine, he has no dreams of any future but a warm cup of tea in the morning, and a little lazy sleep.

No one knows our cause, tonight. Only the three of us, and back in England, Mazzini, I am told. There were two strangers who provided us this boat just a few days ago, but they were paid off, without knowing we were running anything more than the common contraband.

The Captain of that schooner doesn't know any of the dreams that pull these oars beneath his guns.

Suddenly the schooner fired a second shot, as Pilo steered us in toward the shore where the bigger ship could not follow. And that second blast came from a pair of cannon, and this time it was no warning, no announcement. This time they meant to put us on the bottom.

They saw us turn this old fishing boat around and run, so all the warning shots were done. I heard the fierce scream of one shot go over my head, missing our mast by only a few feet. The second shot dropped in the sea just to our fore, and the boat rocked over to the port and then we took on water from both sides, before this true little ship righted herself and held to, though low now in the sea.

I felt the thump of the cannon shot right beneath my feet, and what with the water running on our decks, I was sure she had hit us, and we were taking on the sea. For a moment I was frozen.

"Ahead, lad!" I heard Corrao beller, and it shook me out of my fears. Even in the dark, his bearded face seemed black and square and furious. I was sitting, oar in the water, staring at the waves sloshing across our decks and out at the black sea. "She's bearing for us!" Corrao yelled, and pulled hard on his oar.

I looked up, and there stood the bow of that black schooner, not fifty feet to our port, standing above us like a giant tree, but she was cutting through the water, her sails bellied full, like she was under steam. And she was coming directly at us amidships. By God, they meant to cut us in two, to send our contraband cargo to the bottom, and then fish us out of the seas later, or hunt us down with dogs on the shore. And that would make a night of it for them. And with the way she was bearing at us, there could be no escape.

"Pull harder," Corrao bellered again, and I heard Count Pilo climbing around behind me at the tiller and I put my head down, and drew full on the oar, and I prepared myself for a cold, black swim to nowhere. Nowhere but the black bottom of the sea.

2.

28 March 1860
Ligurian Sea, no sight of land.

Yesterday the light grew too dim for me to continue to write, and it's agreed among us that, with the secrecy of our voyage, we don't burn lanterns or candles at night. Rather than scribble in the dark, I always know that while our weather stays fair, I will have time to write.

How did it arrive that we escaped the black prow of that nameless schooner? I'm not sure I can say. Not being a man of God, I'm not prone to dreams of Providence. But I must confess, it does now seem that some proud fate played into our hands that night, lest we be sunk at the bottom of the harbor now, and never even escape Genova, or even escape a cold and certain death.

As that schooner drove toward us, while Corrao and I leaned into our oars with more than all our strength, the little paranza handled slowly for all the sea we'd taken on.

The Count, I think, pulled hard on the tiller and somehow turned our little boat to the side, the black prow of the schooner slipped past in front of us, catching the tip of our bowsprit and turning us hard in the water, the way old Corrao and I couldn't turn her.

We banged amidships against the schooner, and it took all that I had to hang on to the oar in my hands. I heard the high-pitched whine of seasoned old wood grinding against wood, but not the sound of any cracking or breaking. And far above, the sailors of that patrolling schooner could have shot straight down at us where we sat. But the big ship just sped past. We were so full of water, I guess, we were low and stable while the great schooner was fleet. It swept past and turned us like a little top all the way around in the water. We spun slowly around until the wake of that speeding schooner began to break against our starboard prow.

"Heave to, boys," shouted the Count, as he lifted the tiller high to let the paranza spin. "Heave to, lad," Corrao echoed Pilo.

"Look," Pilo almost whispered in awe, as he set the tiller back in the water, and the breeze gently filled our sails. "Lads, we have come through," the Count shouted then, almost in disbelief, but with great heart.

Off to our port, the schooner sped away from us, her sails bellied full. And we pulled up to cut an angle through her wake, and our paranza headed straight out to sea. "Pull, men, pull," cried the Count. "Pull as you've never pulled before."

I laid into my oar, but I wondered how the Count planned to escape. We were turned now toward the open

24

sea, where surely that quick schooner could hunt us down. Pilo had us headed out away from the shadowy shoreline, and what I thought was our best chance to slip away from them.

I was watching off to our port side as the long schooner began a wide arc to turn around, and I pulled my oar in a heavy rhythm with Corrao. The schooner was moving fast, but maneuvering to catch us slowed her down, and this gave us our main chance. Yet I still didn't see how Pilo thought we could outrun her, once she was righted and on course for us.

I heard Corrao's loud belly of a laugh, and Pilo yelled, "Pull those oars, lads, " as he set the tiller and then he ran past us toward the mainmast right at my back. Corrao was grunting happily with every pull. And this little fishing boat danced over the wake. Above my head I saw what Pilo was about. He was gathering in the sails. It would make us less visible, I realized. We would, without those broad white sails, become a little black shadow moving into the dark of night.

"Don't let up now," Pilo shouted, his arms pulling in the sail cloth. "We're almost through."

I felt a cool gust of wind at my back, and it was filled with a light salty spray, that seemed to mop my sweating brow like a caring hand. I pulled at the oar in my hands until I nearly fell over backwards, but then I lifted her and kept to the rhythm with Corrao beside me.

The schooner, in her wide arc, was parallel to us now in the distance. But she was turned in headed for the shoreline, at that moment going away from us toward the lights of Genova. But I knew once she'd righted herself, she'd be bearing down on us again, but this time with the wind behind her. Count Pilo had made sure of that. I saw that, if my arms and back held out, maybe we could outrun her, even with our paranza taking on all that water.

Count Pilo rose up behind us then. Our two sails were down now, and Corrao and I were the only way the little boat moved in the water. The young Count slapped me on the back, and then he slapped Corrao too, and he laughed a rebellious laugh. "The Gods are on our side tonight, lads," he roared up at the sky. "Pull hard, boys. For Liberta'."

We were moving lithe as a swordfish through the sea, it seemed, the splash of waves on our back, the cool wind drying the sweat on our necks. The strength in my arms seemed then to pull the little boat through the rising seas with a sure ease.

Pilo stepped past us then and took up the tiller again, and he began to guide us straight out into the wind, and out to sea. Slowly, with every stroke of the oar, that turning schooner with all its lights began to grow dim. First it became just a black shadow, with lights casting about, and in just a moment or two I looked up from my hands working the oar to realize the harbor lights of Genova had disappeared in the night.

All around us, with the sea rising and tossing our prow, we had sliced into a mist. A strange blue fog, on the head of some storm, was rolling into shore, into the harbor. And as it enveloped us, I understood what the Count was cheering about. We had escaped into the fog.

With our backs to the ocean, pulling at those long oars, I never saw the bank of fog Pilo was steering for, but I understood as Genova disappeared from sight, this was how he knew we could escape. This was why he'd called out to thank the Gods driving our fate. With the fog growing thicker, and the seas rolling heavy and heavier, we had indeed slipped away into the night, off free and bearing south for the Tyrrhenian Sea.

We will never know how long that schooner searched for us. Perhaps for the whole damned night. Perhaps for just a few moments more. But I don't think she came after us for long. Luck was on our side, and as far as she was concerned, we were just a fortunate band of smugglers. In rough seas and dark fog, that schooner lay close to port, I'm sure, searching for easier prey, prey without so much fickle fortune to bear, prey without some proud Fate pulling the oars along on her side.

I suppose it was the better part of an hour, pulling hard in a rhythm against the waves, my lungs feeling good and strong at the exertion, before my pal Corrao nudged me with the water bottle. "Burtoni, boy, take yourself a drink, by god," Corrao said, pushing my shoulder with the bottom of a black wine jug. "We've done it, lad," he said, with sure finality, "We've done it."

You must understand, Giovanni Corrao is a dark, black man, his head and chin covered with a stark black hair, wavy more than curly. His nose is like a hawk's curled beak under the shadow of a thick squared brow. Out of that darkness, his brown eyes were always lit from behind by a smiling light.

I sat up straight and lifted my oar out of the water, and then I took the bottle from Corrao.

"We gave them the slip," Corrao laughed. "We did!" His head nodded with the swagger of pride.

The bottle was filled with cold fresh water, and while it felt good going down, the water surprised me. I was ready for the fat taste of victory wine in that bottle.

"Hey," I said, "Where's the wine?"

Corrao just laughed some more at that.

"Later, piu piccolo," said the Count from the tiller. "We're not loose of them yet. Not for sure."

So I took another deep swallow of the cool water, and handed the bottle back to Corrao, who was still chuckling as he set it down on the deck between his feet.

I took a deep breath and relaxed a moment, still holding my oar high in the air. That was when I noticed how low in the water the old paranza lay. We were rocking in the rising seas, and when the boat leaned into a wave instead of cutting it sharp, water lapped in and rolled over our feet on the decks, and then seeped into the heart of the little ship. Pilo needed to keep the paranza headed straight into the rolling waves just to keep us afloat.

But though he was only ten feet away, or less, I could barely see the Count in the thickening fog. Even Corrao, alongside me across the deck, faded into the mist a little. The sharp outline of his thick black hair had disappeared into the dark night and the fog.

All around us, as the boat rose and fell in the sea, there was nothing but black water and fog. Since we had not a single light on board, we were essentially invisible. We had vanished into the dim dark sea.

"Rubio," said Corrao. This is the name we call Count Rosalino Pilo now, one of the count's many secret names. "What should we do now, Rubio?" said Corrao.

"Where are we?" I asked, looking all around me at the encroaching mist. I suppose I sounded frightened, forlorn and young.

From the vague shadows that made up the end of our little barque, as it rocked up and down, Rosalino Pilo answered us. "I'll keep her headed into the wind. That wind is blowing in from the sea. You lads row to your heart's contentment, and in the morning we'll come out of this. Then we'll find our way."

Corrao looked over at me, and the light of his eyes told me that I was as vague to him as he was to me. "Ready," he shouted, since it was harder and harder to see. "One and pull," he said, to get us in to the rhythm of our work together.

I set my oar down in the water and leaned back into it, as the boat rolled a bit to the port, and took on more water. Lifting the oar and leaning forward, I noticed a hard, warm wind at my back, and I heard the crash and creak of our prow as it pushed on through the sea.

After a few strokes of the oar, the noise of the water slapping against our ship grew regular and loud. As if to urge us on, out of the fog at our stern, I heard the Count's voice. He began recite the lines of a poem, or perhaps I should say he was chanting them, as if we'd begun some great religious ritual and not some adventure to start a revolution. He sang out these words, out of the dark mist where he'd become a nearly invisible shadow to us.

"Felice te che il regno ampio de venti,
Ippolito, a tuoi verdi anni corrrevi!" he sang.

His voice was high and light, and it drifted out of the darkness, and after just a line or two, Corrao joined him, reciting these ines about heroes of old, lines they both knew by heart, songs of Achilles and his shield and of Odysseus on his wandering ship, and even of the glorious tombs of Dante and Galileo. Then they paused, but we didn't stop the slow beating of oars and the wind swept across the empty mainmast above. Alone, Pilo continued the song, but it was turned now to a lament.

"E me che I tempi ed il desio d'onore
fan per diversa gente ir fuggitivo,
me ad evocar gli eroi chiamin le Muse
del mortale pensiero animatrici."

And then Pilo repeated this line, now singing it over and over as if it was a refrain:

"Chiamin le Muse! Chiamin le Muse!" sang out. "Me ad evocar gli eroi chiamin le Muse!"*

But then Corrao broke back in, singing out to the green years of youth, and to the realms filled with kind winds, and as he sang, Rosalino Pilo joined in again, and slowly the fog around us seemed to lift.

I saw him clearly then, his arm was wrapped around the tiller to hold it steady. He is a small man, Rosalino Pilo, without the heft and size of Corrao. But he clung tightly to that tiller, hugging it to him, and he sang loudly along with dark Corrao.

The mist seemed to move then, away from us, floating away toward the shore, I think. It was like a low night animal, a crouching wolf slipping away into the dark, moving with a suddenness that caught me by surprise.

Still, even with the fog leaching away, and the wind at my back rising, the night was darker than ever. I glanced up as I was pulling back on the oar, and I saw not even one star twinkle in the thick black sky.

---

*It was later that year, once I had returned home to the U of M_____ that my history degree became handy. With a bit of library research and some help from Professor Gianluca Matteo in the Italian Department, I learned that these lines come from "Dei Sepolcri" by the poet Ugo Foscolo (1778-1827). Addressed to Foscolo's fellow poet Ippolitio Pindemonte, the poem sings of the power of tombs to inspire the heroes of the nation. The lines which Burton included in Italian in his text I have roughly translated as follows: "O happy in your green years you roam, Ippolito,/ this kingdom filled with gentle winds. . . . But for me, the times and my hunger for honor/ make me a fugitive in different lands,/ crying out to the Muses for help, calling out to the Muses for heroes!" This, indeed, is what Pilo and Carrao have turned into a refrain: "Call to the Muses! Call to the Muses! Call out to the Muse for heroes!"

"Hold to, my heroes," cried out the Count, trying to warm us, but the end of his words disappeared into the cold crash of a wave topping over us. The water threw me from my seat, and I lost my hold of the oar. For a moment, I couldn't tell what was up or down, for everything was water, and the deck was only something that struck me once on my back and then once on my shoulder. The shock of that second blow made me gasp, and then all I did was swallow long, deep lungs full of sea water. I was sure I was overboard, and I heard the Count's lament for heroes clearly in my head, though I could not find air to breathe, and all my ears could hear was the dizzying rush of water all around. Lost and overboard, I was sure.

3.

29 march 1860
Somewhere in the Ligurian Sea

As I gaze now out at the still sea around me, with our sails slack above us, it is so hard to believe, it seems impossible these are the same waters that nearly swallowed us just a few nights ago. But as we sit here becalmed, I have time again to write it all down.

It was good, fearless Giovanni Corrao, with those thick forearms and heavy shoulders, who saved me. If not for my shady friend, I would have been tossed overboard, lost and drowned by those fearsome waters, lying now at the bottom of this too, too placid sea.

For what seems to me now like an age, like an era, I was topsy-turvy, unable to say even what was up or down in this world, not even knowing what way I should swim to fight for air. But then, suddenly, the flat wooden deck rose up in front of me like a wall emerging out of fog, and it struck me full on in the face. For a brief moment, I felt I could somehow strain to stand up, to find air. If only I could crawl up onto my hands and knees on that deck, I would breathe again. But then the water rose once more, lifting me into the air, or down into the bowels of the ocean, I couldn't tell which. But I felt the deck slide away from me, out of my helpless grasp. I was lost, and I was lost now for good, at last. I could surrender, I could just relax and let this Ligurian Sea carry me away.

But right at that most hopeless of moments, the grasp of a firm hand seized me by my wrist, and out of the swirling confusion, Corrao pulled me toward him. Up, down, sideways, I don't know. But toward him. Soon, somehow, he had an arm swung over one of my shoulders, across my chest and then under the other arm. He hugged me to him, and slowly, as the old fishing boat tossed in those crashing seas, I began to right myself. I caught my wind, first, and then I began to understand up from down, the heavens from the belly of the sea.

Gradually, between the swirls of the waves across the lurching deck, I saw where I was. Giovanni Corrao had lashed himself along with his oar to the railing on the starboard. And from there he'd grasped me out of the waters, and held me with his one free arm against him. He was speaking to me, but it took a long while for his words to make any sense.

When I felt stronger, I tried to squirm free of Corrao's grasp, but he wouldn't let go. He kept speaking to me, and until I answered him clearly, until I spoke, and made some kind of sense, I was deep in his clutches. He would not let me go.

I looked from stern to bow of our little ship, but through the crashing waves I saw not one sign of Rosalino Pilo. These were not clear thoughts, you must know, O Historians and Thinkers of a distant age, they were just a physical realization, as I understood somehow that the Count had been washed away by the sea, just as I would have been, were it not for that grasp of Giovanni Corrao. The paranza bucked through the waters like a tired, worn horse at the end of its longest run. Pitching up at the bow, then plunging down into the sea, with her stern kicked high, trying to throw us off, but only halfheartedly. Mostly she wanted to take on water, and then haul us all to the bottom, toward some watery home.

I can't remember much else, for I lost consciousness somewhere then, a consciousness that deep down in my heart I wearily believed was lost for good.

When I came to, hours later, the ship was dead still on this flat endless sea. Her decks remained wet under the high sun, though slowly I realized the very boards I lay on were dry as sand. It was only the decks to the starboard and the stern that still shone wet in the bright sunlight. And I heard the slosh of water being thrown, in a rhythm steady and strong.

The boat was listing heavily, you see, staying afloat only because of the calm seas, and her old spirit. She'd brought home many a fisherman feared lost and gone in her time. She was trying to do it again.

"Are you sleeping it off?" shouted Corrao's voice.

I lifted myself up, weakly, and turned to look over my shoulder. The oar was beside me, and it was lashed with a rope to the railing, along with my right arm. Corrao had tied me down so I could not roll off into the sea.

I heard his deep laugh at me, "Didn't know what was more important," he said, "you, Burtoni, or that last damn oar." He stopped to laugh again, and I saw him bend at the waist and then stand up again with a bucket in his hand, and toss the water inside it overboard. "So I tied you both down," he said, bending again for another bucket of water.

"Are you well enough to help, lad?"

It was the Count's voice, followed by the slosh of a bucket of water. The sound of it made me crawl up onto my hands and knees, until I could see him. I suppose my mouth was hanging open. Probably I looked like a thirsty dog.

"I thought you were . . ." I said.

But Pilo stood there, at the stern where the sea was trying calmly to lap up over our decks. "If we can bail our little bark out, and let her right herself, we can be back on our way, lad. Trusty little ship, she is."

"Before some other god damned thing blows in on us," Corrao blustered, without stopping his bailing for a moment. "Another damn storm like that last one would send us all straight to the bottom right now."

"Don't worry about that," said the Count, ignoring Corrao. "The skies are clear."

"Yes, and there's not even the breath of a wind for our sails," whined Corrao.

"But are you up to helping us yet, lad?"

I got to my feet on the slanted deck. As I started, then, to untie myself from the railing and the oar, Corrao began to laugh. "Blasted, lazy bones, threw our other oar away." He seemed to increase the speed of his bailing with every word. "Can't be trusted to row, boy, but you sure as hell could lend us a hand bailing her out."

Then, just as I stood up straight, he hit me with a bucketful of sea water.

"Giovanni!" barked the Count. "Overboard. And leave the lad get his feet."

But I had, instead, to try to grab at that last remaining oar, for in untying myself, I'd untied it. And Corrao's bucket of water and insults sent it drifting across the slanted decks, and then off into the Ligurian Sea.

"Damnation," I yelled, as it slipped from my hands and away.

But Corrao just laughed some more, and kept bailing away. "One's not much good, without the other, boy."

The way he calls me boy is a taunt. But he doesn't know my real age, and all that I've seen. He doesn't even know why the Count has me aboard.

When the time comes, I will try to tell him.

So the three of us worked, and that old boat was sound. She was not taking on any water. With every bucket we tossed, she rose up a little in the sea and began to right herself. And slowly the stern lifted and she put her bow back down in the water, and we began to feel stronger and better, singing and whistling and joking on the becalmed seas.

Finally, at one point I was below decks, lifting my bucket up to Corrao, as he tossed the empty down to me, and then threw the new water overboard, when Rosalino strode over to the tiller and gazed down her lines at the bowsprit pointing to the south. Then he stepped over and took a bucket full of seawater from me, as I tried to hand it up to Corrao. "Watch," he said to us both.

I stuck my head up from below, and saw the Count walk gamely over to the ship's prow. She was nearly righted now, and the Count looked back at us. His brown, determined eyes peered straight into my heart. Then he gently poured that bucket of water over the prow, like it was sacramental wine.

"I christen thee," he announced, stentorianly, "La Speranza. The hope of the nation."

Of course he knew what Giovanni Corrao did not, when he named our ship. La Speranza.

And he only knew La Speranza by name because I told him. When the Count found me, hanging around the Genovese port, looking for work, someone had pointed me out to him. I still don't know who, but it could have been anyone. You see, it costs nothing at all, not even half a penny to talk, especially in a harbor town, and everyone has some sort of yarn to tell. Some of them are lies, and some are the truth. But each and every story is bigger and braver than the one just told. Mine, you can be sure, just like you can trust what I put down here in this journal, my tale is all true. All of it.

At any rate, it was early in February, just a few months ago; I met Rosalino Pilo in a tavern by the docks. He called himself Giuseppe Fioratti then, another of his many secret names, and there was no hint that he was a Count from Sicily. He was short and lithe, and he wore his hair long like a revolutionary. He just poured me a glass of wine from the bottle he carried, sat down across the table from me, and said, "People tell me you were in the Anzani Brigade."

I didn't answer. Not even to correct him about the Legion. The way the police are, you don't answer a question like that to just anyone who walks up to you, even with long hair and a free glass of wine. Especially when he's offering a free glass of wine. In parts of this peninsula that are still in the control of the Austrians, just answering that question would make you a criminal.

"Giuseppe Fioratti," Pilo said, to introduce himself.

And so we chatted for a while, about the sea and ships, and then he came around to Switzerland. He lowered his voice, and glanced quickly around the room. "I spent a few years in Geneva, in exile, if you know what I mean. After Rome fell in '49."

I still didn't trust him, since he might have been a spy. And so I thanked him for the wine, and I got up and left.

"I lived in the Republic of Rome, Burtoni." He raised his glass to me, and whispered just loud enough so I could hear, "To the heroes of '49."

But he was strange, and there was a light burning in his eyes that reminded me of my dear old Ciccio Anzani, dead now these ten long years. It was the fire of dreams that I saw in this stranger who called himself Fioratti. And it reminded me of my lost days in Montevideo and of the Generalissimo and our long voyage to Niza, when I learned to read and write. So that I can now put this history down on paper.

So I asked around cautiously and found a few old salts in the harbor taverns, men I knew I could trust, and asked them just who this stranger was that he could know enough to ask me abut the Anzani Legion. One by one, they all grew quiet and cautious. Even though they knew me well, and knew they could talk with me of these things, they were careful and slow. And all they ever told me was that Giuseppe Fioratti was not his real name.

Did that make him a spy or a patriot? In the end, there was no way for me to tell. No one seemed to know who he really was. Or no one felt safe enough to say openly.

That was when I stumbled on Corrao. One night at a stinking hole called Il Gufo sulla Luna he was feeling good and deep into the bottom of his cups, this thick dark man covered with hair, singing loudly in a baritone voice that was as rich as it was flat. He noticed me come in, and before long he had an arm around my shoulders, trying to lead me outside, singing and laughing as we went. But I'd been around enough to know trouble when I saw it, to know the stink of a spy, even if it was singing and offering decent brandy.

So I pulled free of his grip, and tried to walk away. He cursed at me, and then put his paw back on my shoulder, tried to pull me back. I just dusted him off, and you could see the happy drinkers in the tavern squaring up around us, sensing a good tumble in sight. Entertainment for the night, it was. And shaping up nicely, it was, too.

But this drunken fool wouldn't back off. "Burtoni?" he grinned. "It's you? Right? Burtoni?"

I didn't know who the hell he was, or how he got my name, but he put a hand on my shoulder again.

I'm afraid I was tired, and I'd had it with him. I'd already dusted him off once, and I'm a lot older and wiser than I look. I know how to lose a drunk. So I wheeled around, put a fist into his bearded chin, not much, but just enough to knock him down. He did surprise me, how stable he was on his feet though. He seemed drunk, but it took more than I thought it would to set him down.

As I stepped past him and out of Il Gufo into the street, I heard him laughing, as if we'd shared a joke or some such thing. It was only a moment, and I heard his laughter again following me out the door. "Wait, Burtoni," he called out from inside, so I picked up my step.

He caught me a few blocks away, along the docks, breathless and grinning. "Wait, Burtoni, we need you!" he said.

I was about to paste him again, when he held his hands up in the air, and he said, "Il Generale needs you."

I stopped, but I didn't lower my fists.

"Who the hell are you?" I said.

His big grin came back and he stuck out one of those paws, offering to shake my hand, the hand that had just now knocked him on his arse. "Giovanni Corrao," he said, with those same crazy, burning eyes I'd seen in Fioratti. "You sailed with him, from Montevideo, didn't you?"

And that was how this all began.

4.

30 March 1860

We've been stuck drifting for two days now. Our little Speranza is all straight and right, ship shape in the water, but the sea is so still and so glassy smooth after that storm, we simply sit here and drift aimlessly. We, who have such great purposes before us, we drift aimlessly along on the glassy sea. Still this lifeless water gives me plenty of time now to write it all down here. Everything. But it's not getting us any closer to Sicily, with these guns and grenades in our hold. All this sitting and drifting along is beginning to drive me crazy, especially since Corrao has now taken up his singing again. What a sin it all seems.

5.

31 March

Last night, under the clear half moon, a northern breeze drifted in and lifted our sails, and we were by dawn in sight of Corsica. The seas are still and swift, and at last we are making time. By midday we should be through the straights and past Isola d'Elba and on into the Tyrrehenian Sea. Now we are all singing, together, and the seas are flowing with us.

We've not seen another ship since we slipped out of Genova. But that is probably more because of the storm, and the heavy calm that followed it than for any other reason. It will be good to set our course out and away from Sardinia and Toscana, sail into the deepest stretches of the sea and away from the other fishing boats with tongues that wag and too many stories to tell.

Today Pilo and I, under his command, will spend the better part of the daylight checking the muskets. With all the water we took on at the start, they will be in tough shape. And while we were becalmed, none of us had the spirit to care. Dead water deadens the soul, you know, and it is lethal to the dreams of the heart.

But now, today, the fine seas remind us that we may be needing these arms soon, so the Count and I will work, oiling and cleaning, while Corrao guides the paranza through the waters.

6.

1 April
Tyrrhenian Sea
Bound for Messina

The sunset came to end this fine day, and in its last light I saw a distant island. Pilo was at the tiller again, and I wondered aloud to him, "Why are you putting us in so close to shore?"

Count Pilo's eyes gazed past me at the distant shore, and he didn't answer me.

I glanced over at Corrao, leaning forward at the bow again, but he was gazing off to the west as well. "What island is that?" I said.

I knew we were days away from Sicily still. But they didn't answer me, neither one. Their steady gazes told me only that I should know what was out there.

"Sardinia," I said, trying not to sound confused.

"In the distance, yes," Corrao said wistfully. "Beyond," he said.

"Well then, what is this, and why are we cutting in so close to shore? Why do we take the chance?"

As we rounded its shoreline, we sailed up suddenly on a thin line of smoke rising straight up from the dark trees. "There," Pilo whispered, without any gesture other than his direct gaze.

"What is it?"

I thought maybe we were going to put in to pick up more arms, or food, or volunteers, perhaps. But then Corrao looked knowingly back at me and said only one word, "Caprera," and I understood.

No more did he say that name than Pilo cut our little paranza seaward, and I understood we'd had our look. It was straight on now to Sicilia, to Italia.

The time has come this evening for me, at last, to put down here in words the high and true purpose of our voyage. It will be written here, on paper, so that come what may after we land, or between this day and that day when we come ashore, history will have a clear record of us. For it is, indeed, my friends, history we intend to make.

That island of Caprera, with the sun setting over that little cabin, Isola Caprera was our real goal, my friends. You who come after us and read these words must understand.

After the failures of '48, when I ran with him north to Lugano, to escape the Austrian noose. After the Republic of Rome fell in '49, and again the peasants in the countryside failed to rise. And after he left his dearest Anita in a quick and sudden grave in the swamps south of Commachio, by a farmhouse near Mandriole. And then, when the war last year failed, and France and Austria divided up the north between themselves, and Count Cavour made a deal with the French to give away Niza, the General's own home, where his Anita's bones now lay.   After all this, the Generalissimo went home to his little Isola Caprera. He said he would have no more of any of our wars, because enough was enough, and it was clear to him that the common little man, still a slave to the priests and the nuns, would not yet rise up to make a free Italy. And so he was done with it. Until the time was right, until the people were ready, if ever that grave day might come, he was done with it.

"There can be no Italia without him," Pilo said, as our Speranza cut away from Caprera toward the open sea. "Not in our lifetimes," he said. Not even in mine, I wondered, but I didn't speak. "Without him to lead us," Pilo said, hiding all his emotions, "all is lost."

But that, my friend, my fellow patriots, that is why we sail our little hopes across these seas to Messina. There is trouble stirring there on the island of Sicily, trouble for all my years.

"Here is the thing," Pilo had whispered to me, with Corrao looking on, as we three sat with another stranger in a corner of Il Gufo sulla Luna in Genova. "If we can reach Sicilia, with a few guns, and with my friends there . . . "

The stranger had nodded his head as Pilo spoke, and he whispered, "We have friends there."

"If we land there," said the Count, "and bring these guns as a sign, and we tell them that the General is coming, then they will rise up all over the island, in the little villages and in the mountains inland. I know they will, men. They have heart, the Sicilians. They must."

The stranger laughed, and then Giovanni Corrao spoke, leaning forward toward us and nodding his head to the emphasis of his words. "When the General hears that the peasants have revolted, then the General will rise up."

"Yes, he'll leave his little Caprera homestead and he'll lead us," Pilo said, with real fervor.

"And lead the volunteers I'm gathering here in Quarto," the stranger said.

"So, to Sicilia," Pilo finished it. Then the little Count's eyes darted from me to Corrao and back again. He took a sip of wine and he said, "We are the springs in the clock, my friends, and if we are brave and true to our dream, we can set off the alarm, we can rouse up the sleeping giant of Caprera, and then awaken the hearts of all Italia." His fist was closed tight as a seaman's knot, but he dared not pound the table nor raise it in the air. Not yet, and not here.

The stranger, who's name I still have not been told, leaned across the rough table too and he filled all our glasses from the bottle he'd bought, and then he raised his glass to us all. "To Sicilia," he whispered.

"To Italia," answered the Count, pushing his fingers through his long brown hair, and that night we drank to the bottom of that bottle together.

So now, I sit on this deck of the Speranza, knowing that I was chosen by Pilo to be here because of the way the General had adopted me, back in '48. I didn't really know him, it was Anzani who was my friend. We both loved Anzani, and in truth that was why the General loved me.

But it is why I am here. I might just be one more call to awaken the giant, when the General hears that it is I, the

44

one he named Il Rosso at the foot of the Alps, who is fighting for him now in the Madonie and all the way to the Conco d'Oro.

Corrao is singing again, "Felice te che," and Pilo sits quietly at the helm, steering our course, silent as the moon and stars, and our sails are full with the happy winds of our green years. It is only days and we shall see the island, and then know our fates, and with our fate runs the fate of our homeland.

7.

9 April
Straits of Messina

This morning Speranza came within sight of Sicily, and then Rosalino kept us far out to sea. It is afternoon now, and we have dropped our sails and are at anchor, drifting a little in the Tyrrhenian Sea. We must stay alert now. Bourbon ships may be on patrol, and we've had no word now for nearly two weeks. We don't know what is happening on the shore.

We have come to stir up trouble, for we have a little hold full of weapons and we must be wary. There is no way for us to know if we have been discovered.

Pilo, in these last busy days, has told us a little, but in case we are arrested, Corrao and I know only what we must, only this:

There is a man, we know him only as Sole, who is waiting for us in Messina. Sole and his people will lead us into the interior. Sole knows only that a man named Robiolo is coming at night, and perhaps other things we don't know. Once we are organized, I believe, we will begin the revolt, moving along through the villages in the high country. Whether or goal is Messina or on the other end of the island, at the capital Palermo, I can't say. These are things Corrao and I will learn when the proper time comes. When it is necessary, we will learn it, and not before.

I suspect Giovanni many know more than I do about all of this, but he won't speak. And I know there is no point in asking him either. We just press forward with the tasks at hand.

Tonight, we wait for darkness, and then we will slip silently through the Straits and land somewhere to the south on the shores of Sicilia, and we will begin our work to rouse the sleeping giant of Caprera. God speed to us all. Quick departure to all our foes.

For Italia.

II.

There is a break in Jack Burton's journal here. Two blank pages, and a few pages, it is hard to say how many, have been torn out of the leather binding as well.

Rob noticed me pause at those empty pages, flipping them back and forth, touching the torn edges of the missing pages. "So what do you think?" he said. "Am I right?"

I shrugged, and he groaned and laughed at the same time.

"I'm right," he said. "I know I am."

"I don't know," I hedged. "It could be anybody."

"Oh, the hell it could," Rob shook his head in disgust. "Come with me for a walk and I'll tell you all the ways we know it was his."

I understood that Rob was right, but somehow, waiting to believe that this thing was true, that also seemed right. "It's been a long time," was all I said.

"You're damn right it's been a long time," Rob said. "I've been looking for something like this since we were just kids." Rob paused and grinned. "Since he snuck off and left us under the Big Top. Don't you remember?"

"I remember," I said. But I didn't say what I thought then: I'm not as hungry for this as you are, little brother.

The stone streets of Ortigia led us past a few well-lit cafes, and a few shops. Rob navigated like a native, and in moments we were strolling Via Minerva and the Duomo soared above us. Buried in the stone walls, but still visible even in the dusk light, stood tall columns, three stories high, framing the structure of the cathedral. But they were old, older than the Christian church that had swallowed them, they were probably Roman, maybe even Greek, and despite their great age, they seemed stronger and more certain than the masonry of Christianity that had surmounted them. It was as if time, though we put it to use in our lives and our beliefs, in our own history, our personal stories, still the old circular big top of seasonal time stood not just at the root, but even at the fundament and the frame of all our poor but beautiful structures. Our buildings. Our civilizations. Our beliefs.

Though the cathedral was centuries old, and as we rounded the corner and walked into the Piazza del Duomo, those old pagan columns stood to remind us of how temporary we are, even in our greatest ages and our grandest dreams. They were eight, ten, twelve centuries old, we are only standing in the shadow of the temples of the past, and our grandness becomes mere grandiosity.

From the Piazza, we could see the beautiful baroque facade that Andrea Palma had built, with its fine run of stairs, and its swift arches and saintly statues gazing down benevolently at us. But coming at it as we did, those old temple columns, now hidden away, stood firm and upright in my mind.

It made me wonder again about Jack Burton. Nothing about him added up. This strong, burly man in the wheelchair we met one day, fifteen years ago, beside a carnival tent. Nothing about him added up. Telling us stories about his adventures in the Italian Alps a hundred years before, and smoking his funny little pipe. And not this journal, in my hands, tucked under my arm as my brother and I strolled across a Sicilian piazza, telling another yarn, and again a hundred years old. None of it added up. It was

48

all impossible, and I should have laughed at it and ignored it. But I didn't. I didn't do any of that.

"I know it's him," Rob said, and he led us over to a table outside a café, just across the piazza from the façade of the Duomo. "First of all, it fits," he said. "Everything in that book fits with the story he told us back when we were kids. Don't you remember?"

I didn't answer, for obviously my very presence there with him told us both that I remembered.

But Rob took my silence, rightly, for reservations. "And it sounds just like him. Just like the way he talked." He pointed at the notebook that I'd laid now on the table between us. "I swear, I can hear his voice speaking to us when I read that."

"I think you're smelling that funky smoke of his, too." I said.

Rob frowned, and just then a waiter approached, and Rob ordered a liter of red wine.

"That's too much," I said.

"We've got time," he said, and waved an open hand at the old leather book. "You've got to finish the rest of that, 'cause obviously you don't get it."

"Get it?"

"When you finish that, you'll know what I mean. We've got some traveling to do, big brother."

The wine came, with glasses and a little plate of cheeses and salumi, and Rob poured as he said, "Go on, read the rest of it. There's not much more after the break. Besides, you're right at the place where it starts to get really interesting."

As I picked up the old journal again, I conceded, "There is all that stuff about Anzani."

"That's right," Rob settled back in his chair to watch the passeggiatta in the square, and took a sip of the wine.

49

"'Dear Old Ciccio,' remember? That was how he used to say it."

I nodded my head and opened the notebook to where I'd left off. "'Caro Cicio,'" I said, hearing Jack Burton's voice in my head. "But it's impossible," I muttered.

"It's all impossible," Rob agreed, and then held up his glass to admire the dark red of the wine in the evening light. "But it's why we're both here tonight, isn't it?"

What could I do but laugh at that, at the raw truth of it. With my thumb, I felt the nubs of the pages which had been cut out of the old loose binding.

"Go on, read some more," he said. "We've got work to do when you're done, and once you stop doubting everything." He was disgusted.

As my eyes rested on the page, I heard him mutter again, "Impossible." But I couldn't tell whether he was mocking me, or himself.

8.

10 April
Sicilia

Everything has changed now. My lord, I can barely write these words. For everything has changed utterly, the world whole and entire, and all because she was there on the shore. Yes. Rafaella was there on the shore. But wait. I must back up and start from the beginning, from the whole, glorious revolutionary start. So all of History will dare to understand.

Last night after the moon had set, we raised our sails and, without a light on board, without even Giovanni's old pipe, we slipped through the Straits in the dark. To the starboard twinkled the lights of Messina, and off to our port lay the dark shadows of Calabria.

The breeze was light and favorable, so we cut through the quiet water gently, not one of us speaking even one word. It seemed the current of the Straits was with us, forcing us along into the future, pushing ahead, ahead, ever ahead. We saw the grand merchant ships anchored in the harbor of Messina, their lanterns casting lovely shadows on the rippled sea. Once we'd rounded the city at a distance, and made it through the narrows, Corrao headed her back in toward the shores of the island. Pilo stood next to him, and whispered in his ear our bearings, and then the Count would stride up to the bow of the Speranza, pushing a hand back through his long hair, and silently scan the coastline.

It was not long before, in the dark hills to the south, two lanterns shone out brightly for a moment, waived to the right and then to the left in unison, and then went out. Pilo only turned to look back at Corrao at the tiller, and Giovanni nodded. Without a word passing between them, Corrao headed the paranza for that point on the coast.

Pilo waved me over, and then lit our two lanterns, handing me one in silence. I understood. Together, without a sound, we waved our lanterns in imitation of the lights we'd seen on shore. Then the Count gestured with a flat palm across his chest, and I snuffed the flame, as he did the same.

In a moment or two, we saw again the two lights shining from the shore. How many nights, and how many times each night, had they waited for us there, signaling out to the dark sea, hoping against hope that we had made our way? I had no way of knowing. But now at long last, after weeks of sailing, we had come in. It lifted all our hearts on board the ship. As it must have lifted hers too.

That was when, from out of the east behind us, a great battleship appeared. Tall on the sea, and lit with lanterns in rows, she seemed to come roiling out of nowhere. But I'm sure, in the dark, and in our concentration on our dreams of a Sicilian shore, and our search for the signals on the coast, we didn't see her right behind us. But once Pilo and I had lit those two lanterns, we had suddenly appeared out of the dark to the sailors on that war ship.

If she were Bourbon, we were surely done for. We were so close in to her, she could sink us in the night seas. And if not, we surely could not dare to put in to meet our signals now. At the first sound of her cannon fire, everyone ashore would vanish into the mountains, and we would have to make a run back out into the Ionian Sea, to try to slip away into the night before morning light. I don't know that we had enough speed to outrun that great warship and her guns, but we would try. We would sure as hell try.

At that moment, I admit it, I felt tears welling up in my eyes. O, to have come this far, to have slipped away from the Piedmontese in a Genovese fog, to have survived the high seas and then the deadly calm for days, to have found our way here, and seen the shore, to have spotted the clear signal lights, and then only to have our Speranza sent to the bottom by the Bourbon bastards of Naples: It was more than even my old heart could bear.

"Ahoy!" came the call across the waters of the Strait. And then in a moment, the shout followed, "Who goes there?" We were close enough we could see the men on her decks, and she was pulling abreast to put us under her guns. "What vessel are you? Show your flag or prepare yourself for our guns," the voice in the megaphone said.

Pilo looked over at me, and he started to laugh loudly. "Inglese," he said. And I heard Corrao back at the wheel, laughing too.

"Siamo Speranza!" the Count shouted out to the great black warship. Then he turned to me and said, "Tell the Inglese who we are, Burtoni."

I leaned up against the railing and called out, "We are the Speranza!"

"What is your cargo?" the megaphone answered us.

"We are bearing freedom and liberty to Sicily!" I sang out.

There was silence from the English ship. And then the voice in the megaphone asked, "What flag are you flying, Speranza?"

"The tricolore," I shouted back.

"Italia!" shouted Pilo. And then together with Corrao, again, "Italia!"

The English ship sat in the water behind us for a long moment, and then we began to see her turn away, as she showed us her great square helm, like a fine tall building on the water. She sailed away from us then, moving swiftly, but before she'd gone far, a different voice from her decks cried out, without the megaphone to help. "God speed to you, Speranza!" the shout came. And then one great "Huzzah!" rose up from her crew.

God speed, Speranza, indeed.

*   *   *

Near to shore, those lanterns going on and off, led us into a break between two large rocks, and with a hard run we beached our dear Speranza on the white sands. I leapt out into the sea knee deep and held her firm, Pilo was on the other side, then someone from the shore appeared out of the dark and the three of us pulled the Speranza up and firmly onto the beach, as Corrao scurried about, lowering our sails.

Our helper from the shore looked at me, and I saw her grey-blue eyes that seemed bright in the dark. That's right, it was she, dressed in pants and boots, her black hair tied back with a bandanna, knee deep in the water with us. "Rubiolo?" she said to me. Her voice is light and musical. I have sung and even cooed to many a lass, and had my head turned. Never. But this night, standing in the seawater, gazing back into her big eyes, I couldn't speak.

"Sole?" Pilo said to her, from the other side of the Speranza's bow.

She turned away from me to the Count and answered him, "Sole is not here tonight. But I will take you to him." There is a different music to her Italian, there is a curve and a gentleness to it, and it lands too easily on my ear. I was already in danger.

"Va bene," said Pilo to her.

She turned back toward the dark shadows of the volcanic rocks on the shore, and sang out, "Salvatore."

I must stop here. I admit that all of this has nothing to do with the history I am trying to write now. This is not a real and significant part of the record. And yet, I write it down, anyway. You see, with all my years, with the ladies of Montevideo and Nizza and even Genova in my past, with all that, she is different.

There is something about the Sicilian lilt to her words. I hear it too, at times, in Rosalino Pilo, when he is most off guard and at ease. And Corrao, too, had his own gruff twist to his words. But hers is different still. Rafaella, that is her name. You see, from the very first words she spoke, I somehow wanted to hear her say my name with that same sweet Sicilian twist. And something in me was broken, like a shattered oar, when right from the start tonight she turned and spoke to the Count. Right from the start, I wanted to hear her voice. I want to hear it now, and I want to hear her say my name.

This is dangerous.

Rafaella led us up off the beach tonight, with all our cargo in this Salvatore's cart. But I'm still a little confused now, and tired, and as I write this down, so I'm not sure it's making much sense anymore.

Salvatore called her Rafaella. That's how I come to know her name. But I'm not making any sense here. I will try again tomorrow, when I'm not so tired. Maybe it is just I am so tired.

Still I need to write this all down, now, before I forget it. As we followed the cart up into the black volcanic hills, and away from the sea, I looked back down on the lonely shore. And in the not far distance, standing guard over our old fishing boat, and over us I guess, I saw that British ship, at rest and all alight. If there had been time, we might have signaled to them. But there was no time.

So I touched Rafaella on her shoulder, and when she turned those eyes on me again, I just pointed out to sea. She looked from me to the British, and then gave me a nod. We rounded a knob on the hill, and the sea and our true old Speranza were gone, out of sight. She has disappeared into history. La Speranza.

I can write no more.

9.

11 April
From a mountain outside of Messina

This girl, this lovely Rafaella, she brought us here with a two-wheeled cart and a mule. And Salvatore is a little old man, even shorter than she is, and he led the cart out onto the beach, with its big red wheels five feet tall. From there, with few words spoken, we unloaded the paranza and put the muskets and the grenades we have smuggled here into their cart.

And then she brought us here, to where I sit now writing. We are inside a little stone house, and it is morning now. Rafaella is gone, somewhere, and it is time for us to rest, I suppose this is what they mean for us to do. Yet tired as I am, I can't sleep for more than a few moments. The excitement in me makes my heart beat in my very ears. Pounding for he future we have dreamed of, for so many years, it is here. I can feel it, in the air I breathe, in the earth I stand upon. In my heart. It is here.

At first light, I slipped outside to look around, and I can see we are hiding in the hills above the city. The great port of Messina stretches out beneath us, and from here we can look out on the Straits. In the distance, past the ships sailing calmly through toward the Mediterranean, lie the shores of Calabria, clearly in sight.

Corrao and Pilo are asleep, and Salvatore's wife, she calls herself Ada (I don't know who is using a true name and who a false), is moving about the little cottage. When she sees me writing here in the morning sun, she brings me coffee and a chunk of crisp and simple bread, like a cracker, and a chunk of some pungent, salty white cheese.

Moments ago I asked her where Salvatore was, but I am in trouble. I was really just trying to discover when lovely Rafaella will return. I can still see her now, in my mind's eye. I wonder, is this her true name? Rafaella.

Last night, when we all arrived here, she did not come inside straight away. Salvatore introduced us to Ada, and Ada showed us where to bed down. But Rafaella disappeared with the two-wheeled cart full of weapons and ammunition off somewhere back into the hills behind the house. So we were seated inside around a rough table, Pilo and Corrao and I, with Ada dishing out a plain hot soup for us, when Rafaella slipped silently back into the warm room. I almost didn't notice. Almost.

"Hidden?" asked Pilo.

She nodded yes. And then, in that light of the kitchen fire, I truly saw her for the first time. She looked around at all of us, one at a time, sizing us up I suppose at that rough table.

Her nose is little and round, with a tiny little upturned point, and her mouth beneath it is full and wide. Her lower lip is plump and lovely. It is her eyes that make me catch my breath though, for they are a shining gray, in almost any light, and they are wide and intense. They are not like any other woman's eyes I have ever seen. And she looks at you straight in the eyes, too, unlike most of the rough girls I've known. I'm afraid, this one, she seems to see straight into me then, with those deep gray eyes, and somehow I can't bear it and I can't look away. I have not been shy and tongue-tied like this around a woman in years, many years.

I am in trouble.

Ada handed her a glass of dark wine, and Rafaella drank it down in one long draught. And then came the truly remarkable thing. At least beyond her dancing eyes. You see, she took the sky blue scarf from around her brow, and with one shake of her head, turbulent curls of long black hair fell loose and all around her oval face. Her hair is like a beautiful dark cloud around the moonlight of her face. And clouds seems to move and develop around her, so black they are almost blue in the soft warm light of the kitchen.

There is news, and I must get back to this history. You see, Rafaella returned late this morning, or rather this Sole finally came to meet us, and she was with him. And this comrade called Sole was bringing news.

I must write it down here, for the record, lest I fall off the trail of my history. Let me start over: It was late when they arrived, and Pilo and Corrao were up now and rested. But we are all three of us restless. We have not come this far to hide out in a peasant's house and watch the Neapolitan ships drift by below on the Straits. We have come to act upon the world and to make a change.

And what Sole told us then only made our restlessness more unbearable.

"The revolt has started," he said. He's a short man, this Sole, but lean and hard and he sports a startling shock of grey hair from his head, thick and fierce, even though it is close cropped. His beard in straight white, cut short as the hair on his head, and all the hair frames his dark tanned face. But he is not dark from hours of hard work in the sun on land or sea, like Salvatore is dark, like Giovanni and I are dark. His skin is smooth and supple, plump and rosy as a girl's. But it is dark, and his gray eyes sparkle inside this frame of silvery white hair. Perhaps it is that silver hair that makes his face seem so shaded.

Pilo sits up straight at the word of this revolt, and Corrao is immediately on his feet. The time has come. It is now, we think. The Sicilians are at the ready. We are ready.

But Sole raised his hand, like a priest, and said, "My friends, it is not going well." Then with a grand gesture, Sole sat us all back down around the table.

I sat on the bench seat then, to be next to Rafaella, and I was a little startled to sense how small she was. Suddenly she seemed frail and vulnerable, not the way she seemed before. Last night she was short and intent, filled with power and confidence. Today she is just tiny and frail. Her hair was bound up again, this time in a blood red scarf, and she folded her hands as if in prayer, and set them on the table while we listened to Pilo and Sole talk. This is the first time I have seen her clearly in daylight. Now her lovely eyes are not so startling, but the shape of her face, the beautiful cut of her high cheekbones and the pale freckles across her cheeks, they still leave me speechless. Her gaze is completely locked on this Sole, though. She seems indeed to dote on his every word, and I don't know yet what to make of that. Is it patriotism I sense in her eyes and the fold of her little hands, or is it something else? He, on the other hand, seems to ignore her, to take her for granted.

"They rose up on the fourth," Sole said. "But their plan was discovered. Somehow. Francesco Riso, a stone mason from Palermo, he is a brave man, I have known for many yers. And my friends Riso has led the peasants and the citizens of the city, but somehow their plans were discovered."

"How?" asked Pilo, frowning.

"No one knows, Rubiolo. Or at least none of us knows." Sole said, "But I do know this, my comrade. We must be careful and we must not trust anyone, because someone gave up Francesco Riso and his men. I do know this, that spies and turncoats are everywhere."

"What happened?" Corrao asked.

"The plan was to gather just before nightfall at the Gancia. The Gancia is an old monastery in the city," Sole said, looking over at me. He understood that Pilo and Corrao know Palermo well. "They had arms and ammunition hidden there, at the Gancia, and Riso the mason was to meet there with twenty or thirty men. At dark they would take to the streets and begin the revolt. The city would rise up; the Palermitani would revolt and drive out the Bourbons. Palermo would declare herself free, just as she did back in the days of the Vespers. And again that would be the beginning of a free Sicilia."

Sole stopped there, for a moment he lowered his head and he placed his dark forehead in his hands and stared at the tabletop. Rafaella unfolded her hands and she put one on Sole's shoulder, to comfort him. It was a gesture that meant they were close, they were familiar. Perhaps they were even more than that. This I'm afraid was hard news for me, and my heart was sinking, and sinking, simply at the touch of her hand on another's shoulder. I told myself that it was the failed revolt that worried me, but I was lying to myself.

"Lombardo," Salvatore whispered, trying to comfort him. I think he was using this Sole's real name, a mistake, but one that was safe with us, I knew.

"What happened?" Pilo asked again. "Sole?" he repeated, when this secretive man didn't answer.

I noticed it was Ada who spoke first. "Lombardo and Riso are old friends in the society," she said to the three of us. "They are like fratelli. They are men of honor."

"Riso is tough, Lombardo," Salvatore whispered to him. "He will be all right."

Rafaella stroked this Lombardo's shoulders, and he slowly raised his head up from his hands, looked at her and then he went on proudly. "The soldiers arrived at Gancia before dark, and they knew who and what they were looking for. They seized the monastery, they tied up the monks in two's and three's, and then they ransacked the building."

"And Riso?" Corrao said.

Lombardo looked over at him. "He is in their prison, I fear, my comrade." The man we called Sole paused, and it had a dramatic effect, his silence falling on all of us. "I am sure he is being tortured by them, as we speak right now. But Ciccio Riso is brave, he bears a true heart within his breast. He is a man of honor. He will not give up any names. You can be sure."

Pilo slid over to one side in his chair, as if he were about to rise up. "And the revolt?" he said, impatient to return to the point.

Lombardo turned slowly, looked him directly in the eyes, and he said one word, "Crushed." But he seemed defiant when he said it, not defeated. There was something vicious and cornered in his eyes. I understood he could be dangerous, not one you could safely cross, and my heart sank even lower then. I was already, I'm afraid, planning to cross him.

"It can't be over," Pilo met his straight gaze with the same hunger and defiance.

"Oh, there are some squadre left, contadini from the hills, who creep down into the city at night, take a few shots and then disappear." Then Sole gazed over at Pilo. "But they won't last. There's no organization, Rubiolo. The revolt is broken. And when the crops start to come in, then these men, these contadini will be needed at home, back in the mountains, and then the squadre will just vanish. They'll disappear without a trace. And with them goes our revolt, Signor Rubiolo. That's the end of it. I'm afraid, my friends, you have traveled far through many dangers, only to arrive too late. It is what always happens here, on our cursed island. It is over, Rubiolo. Over, I say."

Then a dark shadow covered his lowered eyes, and Rafaella put an arm around him, moving her body toward him and away from me where I sat, dumbly listening to all this black talk. The blackness of heart filled the morning light.

I thought Salvatore might curse at these words of Sole's, but before anyone else could respond, Count Rosalino Pilo sat back in his stiff wooden chair, threw back his head, tossed his long hair like a mane, and laughed out loud. All of us were frowning at him then. The Count paused, he looked quickly at Giovanni Corrao and then over at me, to keep us silent, to make us complicit in the lie he was about to tell.

"No, my dear Sole," he said. "All is not lost. We will, indeed, make Italia this time."

Lombardo lifted his head in disbelief, and he was about to object. "Rubiolo," he muttered, but Pilo cut him off with this simple statement.

"He is coming, Sole." There was a moment of profound silence while everyone in the room digested Pilo's lie. He let his glance briefly land on Corrao and on me again, to be certain we would stay quiet. "That is why we are here, Sole. To prepare the way for him, and to pass the word, so that everyone is ready. All these peasant squadre in the hills, and the laborers in the city streets. Everyone. Because he is coming, with thousands of volunteers from the north, and with ships filled with supplies. Do you understand? He is coming."

I ventured a glance over at Corrao, and I found he was looking back at me, his face like a stone, but our eyes were big with the deceit when they met.

"The General will come?" said Salvatore, in disbelief.

Pilo is a great liar. He didn't even crack a smile as he said, "We've come to pass on this word, Sole? We've come to prepare his way." I noticed that Count Rosalino, while he stretched an arm out to indicate the three of us together, the "General's advance guard," he was careful not to look either Corrao or me in the eye.

But this Lombardo, who calls himself Sole for the cause, he is cagey. Before he would show any excitement or even any interest, he wanted to know the facts, "When?" He leaned forward just a little over the tabletop, toward Pilo, and Rafaella's arm dropped away from him, hesitantly. I can't help it, I felt my heart lift. Probably, it showed in my face, and it made our lie about the General seem more true than the truth. "Where is he landing?" Lombardo asked, his eyes seeming hungry again.

She brought her tiny hand back to the table, but she didn't fold them together like before. It was just an impulse.

63

Without thinking, I reached over with my big paw and I held both of hers in my hand, and gently squeezed them. Our eyes truly met for the first time. Hers spoke simply, 'Is it true?' I'm not sure at all what mine were meant to say. They made me forget Lombardo's strange intensity. I'm afraid they made me forget everything. I am already deeply in trouble.

Rosalino Pilo was clever, though, and his answer to Lombardo was direct. "There are spies, everywhere, Sole. You said so yourself."

Lombardo nodded yes, knowingly. Rafaella squeezed my hand back and then drew away, but her gaze lingered on mine for a moment or two longer, and like a child my heart beat harder then. But I am an old man, despite the way I look. I am not an innocent child.

"What do we need to do?" Lombardo said.

Pilo gave out a list of orders then, and most of it, though I was looking straight at him and trying to listen closely, I don't remember. As my heart beat in my chest as if I was running a race, these men laid out the plans. Most of the guns would stay hidden, with Salvatore and Sole, until they were needed. Pilo and Corrao and I would travel overland, through the villages along the way to Palermo. We would spread the word, we would plant the seeds of revolt and prepare the way for the General's arrival. And there were many other plans laid out across that table today, but they have all disappeared from my memory because I heard just one thing: Rafaella is to be our guide.

Ada said something to Rafaella then. I don't know what it was. But she got up from her place at the table and went outside with Ada. Pilo and Lombardo just continued to talk, and Salvatore and Corrao were joining in, but as I sit here and write this down now, I can only say there were some disagreements about how we should travel across the island. What was the best and safest route for us to take? Which villages would be most ripe to hear our message? But to me it was all only a list of names, one town after another, and none that meant anything to me. I've never been here before, so to me one town sounds like another.

So after awhile, I got up and I followed the two women outside. I found them sitting down the hillside in the afternoon sun, on a bench with a basket of oranges between them, talking and peeling away the rinds slowly. As I approached them, they fell silent, and suddenly Ada stood up. I don't know why. She made a few weak excuses, grinning broadly at Rafaella, and then she left.

Rafaella handed me a little round orange, and gestured for me to sit on the bench beside her, with the basket of sweet fruit between us. Her fingers were stained pink with the juice of the orange. She pulled a section loose and handed it to me, and its flesh was a deep red. "Have you tasted these before?" she said.

Sweet, but with a cutting bitterness buried beneath the sugar, that orange was the best I have ever tasted. I told her so.

"Salvatore and Ada grow them, down there," she pointed down into the walls of the valley below us, away from the sea.

I can't tell you now what I said. O, I can hear her voice in my mind, singing, and I think we talked a lot about how brave it was of her, to lead us across the mountains. I know she said that I was very brave to come this far, across the ocean, to help free an island I'd never even seen before. I answered with just one word: the General's name.

It surprises me now, when I think of it, but Rafaella didn't ask me anything about the General. In the past, whenever his name crossed my lips in conversation, it had always led to "Do you know him?" and then to a string of questions about him that make me just disappear into the thinnest air. And there is not one question among them all that I don't take great pride in answering. It is a great and even boastful joy to be able to say you know him.

But not Rafaella. And not this afternoon. She seemed to take it all in stride, unshaken by the General's great fame, or my closeness to him. With her, this is all so refreshing, like the red orange flesh in my hands. Instead of talk about the General, she told me about a place we would go to soon. It was her favorite place in the world, a little village high up in the mountains, with a view of Mount Etna,and a sharp cliff that drops to the sea, and groves of almond trees and grape vineyards on the steep slopes, and an old stone villa high on a rock overlooking it all.

"When I was a little girl," she told me with her grey eyes shining, "I would spend the summers up there in my father's little house. I'll take you up there. When we reach that place, someday soon."

"What's it called?" I asked, mainly just to keep gazing at her and listening to her voice.

"I used to help when we harvested the grapes and then we'd make the wine and put it away in barrels. And my Nonna would make her almond cake, and in the long summer evenings, we'd have a glass of wine and a big slice of her sweet cake, drizzled with honey from the bees on the mountainside."

"Where is this place?" I asked.

"There is an English family there now," she said, probably because she could hear the accent in my speech. "They own the villa now, or it seems they do, and they live up in the castle on the rock. The Duke and Duchess of Brumonte."

"I'm not English," I told her.

"They're really very nice, Burtoni," she said my name, and the sound of it echoed around in my chest, almost making it hard for me to breathe. How can I be so lost so soon, like a little boy with his first love. "I think you will like them, especially the Duke. The Duchess is a little, oh, you know. She knows she is a Duchess."

I took her hand again, this time it had a red orange in it, and her fingers were sticky with the juice. I wanted to kiss them clean. "Please," I said. "I want you to call me by my name. Call me Jack."

"Jack," she said, though in her mouth it came out like "Jaaqquo," and that made me laugh.

"Rafaella," I said.

"I like Burtoni better," she said.

"Burtoni is fine."

But then she took another try at "Jack," and laughed at herself. Her laugh tinkled like the magic of little church bells at early morning mass.

"Burtoni is fine," I said.

"Rafaella," we heard a deep voice call out, and when we looked up we saw Lombardo and Pilo, two short men striding vigorously down the hill, their arms working like pumps, their chins held up, stiff and strong in the air. But Lombardo seemed to be in a hurry, even more in a hurry than Count Rosalino.

"Cara Rafaella," Lombardo ordered. "Take this and post it with the English in the harbor, dear." He handed her a sealed letter, and his name for her lingered in my ear. I could see the letter was written in Rosalino's hand, but I couldn't make out to whom it was addressed, yet Lombardo seemed to place great importance on it, and on its swift delivery. So clearly he was leaving it in the hands of someone he could trust.

"Hurry back here tonight, cara mia, and be careful," he turned from her to Pilo. "She can lead you out of here, after dark."

"We'll be ready," I said, and the two men seemed a little startled that I was speaking. But I was looking again into Rafaella's eyes, and I didn't care what they thought. Lombardo took her in his arms again, and she looked away from me. With a gentle embrace, he whispered something in her ear, then he kissed her cheek and held her at arm's length. "Be careful, but hurry back," he said. "Come to me, when you return, all right, my dearest?"

From that moment on, I could not catch her gaze. She would not look back at me.

After she was gone down to Messina, Lombardo spoke something in Sicilian to Salvatore, being careful that neither Count Pilo nor Corrao heard it. He made a point though of letting me hear, since he knew I couldn't understand. He needed to remind me, for some reason, that I was just another foreigner. Then he left in a rush, away in a different direction from where he had sent Rafaella.

Ada led us to a small bedroom, and showed us where we could rest until dark. Corrao stretched out on the one bed, but my heart was still beating and my eyes were wide as open windows on a summer night, trying to let the coolness of rest in. But even if I tried, my eyes would not stay closed.

"Who was that letter for?" I asked, as soon as the three of us were alone.

Corrao, on the bed, let out a hardy guffaw and then rolled over on his side with his back to us, in order to try to sleep. "While you were off with the lovely signorina," he muttered, "Rosalino put on quite a show."

"Watch your tongue, Giovanni," Pilo snapped. "We don't know who might be listening to us."

Corrao guffawed again, "Ol' Rubiolo, indeed," he said, and then snorted himself into a more comfortable position as he settled on the bed.

"Who?" I asked again. I was stretched out on the floor with a straw pillow under my arm, leaning over toward where Pilo sat on the floor beside me.

Pilo said, with a face of absolute stone, "I wrote to il Generale to tell him the revolt has begun."

"But?" I said, and Pilo slid closer on the floor next to me, with his eyes on the door out into the little kitchen where we'd just eaten.

"He's playing the great game, Burtoni," muttered Corrao, with his back to us. And he spoke ever so softly, beneath his breath.

Then Pilo whispered quietly to me, " The General wants to know that the people have risen up in revolution before he will once again commit himself to the fight, correct?" His glance rested on the open door a moment, and then Pilo spoke even more softly. "The Sicilians are afraid to rise up without Il Generale to lead them on into the fight. So, you see, we will just give them both the little push they want. Tutte a due."

"We'll do what?"

"I wrote to tell the General the revolution has begun. So now he will come. And for the next few weeks, Burtoni, it is our job to tell the people of this island that the General is on his way, whether he is or not. You see, this is what I plan. We'll stir up this revolt, the three of us, everywhere we go all across the island, so it makes enough noise to bring on Il Generalissimo himself. He won't be able to stay away."

Corrao couldn't help but chuckle, even if he was trying to ignore us and sleep. "Brilliant," Corrao muttered, sounding content in a way. He is enjoying the trick in it all, he is. Giovanni Corrao, you see, he loves to be on the inside of any little game we might play.

"But you told me in Genova . . . "

Pilo broke it off, just to silence me. With a shush, he went on, "I told you just what I told Il Generale. And now, my friend Burtoni, it is up to you and brother Carrao and me to make it all come true. Every story I've told. We'll make them all true. "

"But what if . . ."

"There are no 'what if's' now, Comrade Burtoni. It is up to the three of us to make my little words become the God's truth. And then," Pilo sat back against the bed, and took out paper and ink, "then together we will all make Italia." He held up just one finger in the air. "Italia will be one. But the beginning rests with the three of us."

I started to speak, but he showed me an empty hand, then, and said, "Now, I need to write a few more letters, and you, my friend, you need to get some rest. Little Rafaella's pretty eyes, or not."

I glanced over at him sharply, but he just grinned at me like an elf. "Get some rest, lad," he said. "You will need it, soon enough."

And yet I couldn't sleep, and so instead I have written all this down. And soon Rafaella will return. Pilo tells me now to put this away, to get some sleep before nightfall. It is an order now. I'm not a sailor or even a rebel anymore, he says to me. I'm soldier.

But waiting for her, how can I sleep?

10.

14 April
Randazzo

O these Sicilian hills are a hard, hard country, filled with scrabble and dust even in the spring, and especially when we travel at night. The horses, not fine ones by any means, are slow and the roads at their best are just wagon ruts in the dirt, peppered with stones. So the horses step along slowly and precariously. There is only the four of us. Most of the time, Rafaella leads the way, because she is the one among us who knows the way.

When daylight came, on our first morning, the 12th, we were still miles from anywhere. But it was not Rafaella's fault, or the fault of these old horses we ride. It was our narrow escape from Salvatore's house that put us behind.

That first night here in Sicilia I had finally fallen asleep, when suddenly Ada was shaking me, but she had her hand covering my mouth. ""Shh!" she whispered, into my face. The room was black with night, and she led us quickly crawling out the one window in the room. Salvatore was right outside, and carrying our few things with us, we scurried across the dirt farmyard following him to a long, ramshackle shed, and inside it were these four old horses, the same horses we are riding now.

Without a word, Salvatore led us in beneath those horses in the narrow stall that was really built for just two animals. And then with his hands he covered us with straw. I was still disoriented, not really awake enough to know what was happening, and the night air was cold. Behind me, I could sense Pilo and Corrao, but we made not a sound. None of us. And the smell of the manure was ripe and fresh, because we were lying in it.

That was when I felt her hand reach over and take hold of mine, just the way I had held hers at the table. She whispered almost soundlessly, like a breath, and I felt it on my cheek more than I heard it. "Soldati," was all she said.

We lay still for the longest while, and I wondered how we would know when it was clear. They must have found the Speranza. Surely the British would not have turned us in. But I heard Lombardo's and Pilo's words echoing in my mind. 'The spies are everywhere.' And I knew, just as Pilo and Corrao did, that if we were captured, it would be a quick firing squad for us, and the end of Sicily's dreams of the General's arrival. So now, even to breathe seemed a chance.

There was a clatter of horses and the sounds of several men running outside. Then I heard Lombardo's voice. "What do you think you are doing?" A few men called in the distance, and I heard Ada cry, "Stay out of there."

That led to a lot of crashing around in the distance, and the boot stomps and called orders moved past us in the night.   It may have been my sleepyheadedness, but all of these alarms came and went quickly, swooping back and forth outside, roving through the night.   Then there was quiet for a while, and it went on for a long, long moment. I grew restless, and the stench of that crowded stall was growing old. I started to move my legs, but immediately Rafaella's hand tightened around mine, and just her touch told me to lie still, that Salvatore or Ada would tell us when it was safe to move, when we might escape.

Suddenly, out of the night, I heard a sharp voice threaten, "Where are they?" Then there was a loud slap, and the sound of feet scuffling in the dirt. "Where are they?" the man's voice shouted shrilly now, and I heard Ada crying.

"Keep your filthy hands off of her," Salvatore threatened right back. And then, just outside the shed, there were the scuffling sounds of men wrestling.

"That's enough," Lombardo's voice said calmly.

"What's in here?" the shrill officer said, speaking now, but without much breath.

"Go on in and see for yourself," spat out Salvatore. "Spaniard," he added with scorn.

But Lombardo spoke calmly again, maybe too calmly. "It is just their stable, Bosco. Go Ahead. Take a look for yourself. See what you can find."

"I will," this Bosco said, crisply now.

The door creaked open on its rusted iron hinges, and Lombardo said from outside, "Just a few old horses in there, Commander Bosco. What are you looking for?"

"You know who I'm looking for."

"Really? And who might that be, Signor Bosco?" The vivid strain of insult in Lombardo's voice told me how well he knew this Bourbon Commander.   He knew him well enough to understand exactly how to get under his skin.

I lay still, not even breathing at that point. I felt isolated then, trying to sense Pilo and Corrao behind me, and despite Rafaella's hand curled in mine, I felt alone.

"Why so many horses?" Bosco asked, and some soldiers, three or four of them, stomped in. The bayonets were set on their rifles, I knew without seeing.

"Salvatore keeps some of mine in his pasture," Lombardo lied easily. "The bay and the black mare are mine, Commander, sir?"

This Bosco laughed, and tried to sound as insulting as Lombardo did. "Nice horses, Signor Avvocato." Then the Commander jerked a hand at his soldiers, "Go ahead."

"That old mare there, I've had her a long time," Lombardo kept lying, and now he acted defensive about his animals. "Don't make fun of her, she's a good horse, Signor Bosco."

The soldiers began to fork through the straw and manure with their bayonets. I wanted to scream at them, then. I wanted to hurl myself over Rafaella to protect her. But what I wanted wasn't what I should do, and I knew it. The smart thing was to be still, and I did the smart thing.

The soldiers, pushing around in the manure, stirred up the horses, and they began nervously clomping around in the tight stall. Behind me the big brown bay stumbled, its back feet losing their grip, so he reared up a little. He had stepped on Corrao's shin, but I didn't know that until later. All four horses bumped against one another, and they snorted and reared back their heads. Their restlessness slowed the three soldiers down to a pause. That's when the big black mare lifted her tail, and she spouted out a stream of soft, grassy shit, followed by the long fluting song of gas. The clumpy shit landed right on my shoulder, and it was loose enough to slide down through the straw and onto my arm. Her gas was acrid and bitter, and it filled that little shed so everyone in it could taste the inside of her stomach in the back of their mouths. "That mare is sick," one of the soldiers moaned, his accent bore a hint of Spanish.

"We better separate her out, Salvatore," Lombardo said from the doorway, "or the others might get ill too."

The mare, as if she'd been trained, let fly with another hissing vent of gas, and then she snorted.

"Let's get out of here," Bosco said. And his soldiers happily complied, as the bunch of them backed out of that little doorway.

We all lay completely still for the longest time, waiting for Bosco and his Bourbon soldiers to be truly gone, wary of some trick, some quick return of the bayonets we'd so narrowly escaped.

Rafaella's hand slipped away from mine, and I felt even more alone. I suppose I must have sighed or grunted or something, without knowing it. But that was what started it, for I heard Giovanni Carrao start to laugh, and then stifle himself. But that only started Count Pilo, and then Corrao couldn't help himself.

"That sweet old horse sure got us out of a pile of shit," Corrao whispered.

"Maybe you," Pilo answered, and at that, even Rafaella began to laugh at me.

So I sat up out of the straw, looked around me in the dark stall at these mounds of hay, jiggling with laughter, and I said, "It's not funny."

But then Rafaella pushed the straw away from her face, and I realized that she had taken her hand away to escape the horseshit that was drooling its way down my arm. I saw her grin, and I saw the trembling of her shoulder in laughter. The grassy clumps of shit had run now from my neck down my arm and into my lap, and the relief of our narrow escape showered over me then, and I too began to laugh, louder than all the rest of them.

"What's this horse's name?" I asked, and patted our savior on her sour, stinking ass.

"She's Joan of Arc," answered Rafaella.

I started to laugh again at that noble name, when Pilo grabbed my arm—the one that was soaked in Joan of Arc's shit—and he pulled me back to the ground. A flurry of straw covered me again, and I heard Corrao utter a quick, "Shh!"

Outside there were footsteps running quickly toward the shed. We didn't hear the rattle of any boots or guns, but in the distance there was the rattle of scattered gunfire, and strange, almost human screams. It was followed by a string of curses the like of which I'd never heard before on any ship, in any battle, even from those veterans of the bloody wars of Argentina. What's more, it was a woman hurling out that language.

There came a long silence after the gunfire, followed by the sound again of struggle just outside the shed. "Leave it be," Salvatore said. But Ada answered him with another jolting stream of profanity, but in Sicilian now, so I know it was profanity only because of the way that she spoke it.

We all breathed easier when we recognized those voices. The iron hinges creaked again, and Salvatore and Ada stepped inside, closing the door quickly behind then.

"Let's go!" Salvatore said, whispering loudly. "Presto! Before they come back."

Without another word, we all rose up and in a few moments those four horses were saddled and all our things were packed on them. "Take the road through the mountains to Novara," Salvatore told Rafaella. I heard her whispering back and forth with Ada in Sicilian, but there was no time then to ask what was happening.

In moments we slipped off down into the trees at the edge of the house, on those four old horses. Rafaella was at the head, leading us without a light visible. I am on Joan of Arc, as seems fitting. And I brought up our rear, more to keep me downwind than anything else. None of us were smelling too fresh though, after hiding in that stall and bearing up under Joan of Arc's heroic waste. I heard nothing, saw nothing of the Bourbon troops, and both Ada and Salvatore disappeared back toward the little house without another word, not even a farewell.

It was only later, this morning by the stream, that I clearly understood what had happened. Lombardo had led Bosco and his troops off to the next peasant's house in these hills with reports that we'd been seen there, and we had slipped away in the opposite direction, hoping not to be noticed until we'd vanished into the rugged mountains.

"How did they know we were here?" Pilo asked.

Rafaella shrugged.

"Someone talked about us," Corrao said bitterly, " in the wrong places."

No one answered him, or said anymore about it. We could have been seen by dozens of locals, and we all knew it. But we also knew the truth that spies were everywhere, and it was impossible to know for certain whose side anyone was on. Except for the three of us, and Rafaella. She too was one of us now.

"What was all that gunfire?" I asked, "and those screams?"

"Commander Bosco, when he couldn't find us, he had his men shoot all of Salvatore's pigs," Rafaella said.

The sound of those screaming animals will stay with us all forever, I believe. "There'll be some butchering to do today," said Pilo, trying to show a stone cold humor.

There was silence, and no one wanted to laugh.

"And in the future, too," Corrao muttered, hate spilling from him out into the night.

"We'll have none of that, Giovanni Corrao," Pilo said, sounding off orders now. "We're not here to butcher anyone. We've come with freedom in our dreams. There's no place for revenge in our revolution, Brother Corrao. No place. No place at all."

Corrao was silent through Pilo's little speech, but when the Count was finished, just a beat too late, he said, "Yes sir, Rubiolo."

Night approaches now, and soon we will be off again after dark toward a village called Novara di Sicilia, I have been told. It is a town, according to Pilo, where the seeds of revolution are ready to sprout. How we know this, I am not sure, but still it is the direction where Rafaella leads us. As I write this down, Pilo is again working on something of his own, though I don't know what it is. Tomorrow we truly begin, he says, so he tells us over and over to rest, but to remain watchful. This is how each of our days will go now, at least until the revolution itself begins. We will sleep the afternoons away, in almond groves like this one in the high country, and tonight we will make our way on to Novara. But at this moment Rafaella sleeps peacefully beside a large stone fence, with the common, gray-green cactus scattered all around her. When her eyes are closed, she seems helpless and a child. But we have all seen her move through the dangerous night with great courage and with a true heart. She is far, far from helpless. She is no child, however she seems in her sleep. I want to protect her from every danger, I know. But it is a protection she doesn't need.

What does she need?

I must stop now. I must try to sleep.

11.

15 April
In the Peloritani above Novara di Sicilia

Yesterday, once we had stopped in the daylight, Rafaella washed our clothes. She had been sleeping amongst the flowering cactus, and Pilo was writing still. I put this journal down and was trying to sleep when she suddenly walked up, knelt down with one knee next to me, and with a hand on my shoulder, she said "Burtoni, give me your clothes."

I thought for a moment I was dreaming, my chance had come, but then she handed me her blanket, the one she'd been sleeping in moments before, and she walked over to where Corrao was sleeping near the horses.

I climbed out of my filthy shirt and pants, still decorated by old Joan of Arc, and I wrapped Rafaella's blanket around me. Pilo was still writing away, but she took his shirt from him, and she collected Corrao's clothes too, where he was sleeping soundly near the horses.

She carried away our clothes down into a narrow, carved gully, and out of our sight. In the warm spring sun, lying under her blanket without my clothes, the smell of the damp earth mixing with the warm scent of Rafaella in the blanket, I fell soundly, soundly asleep.

It was late in the afternoon when I awoke, feeling a little chill. Pilo was sleeping now finally, and Corrao was deeply asleep, his head resting on his saddle. Rafaella was nowhere to be seen.

So I got up and with her blanket wrapped around my shoulders, naked as a baby except for my boots, I tromped down into the gully where she had disappeared with our clothes.

The old ground was rocky, but rich and black with volcanic soil, and all around spread a strange mix of grass with cactus and brush on the hillsides. There was a trail, yet it was not easy walking. But as I wound down through that notch, it opened out into a fine mountain stream, clattering along over mossy rocks beneath the cactus dotted hills. I heard Rafaella humming and singing in Sicilian before I saw her. She was sitting in the sun, her bare feet beside the stream, with her toes dangling in the water.

My clothes, and Pilo's and Corrao's, were spread out across the grey green brush, drying in the hot sun on the hillside above her. She had her sleeves rolled up above her elbows, and her long hair was bound up in a knot made of itself on top of her head. She was so lost in the sun and her song, she didn't hear me approaching.

I said her name, a magic charm it was, and she looked up, not startled, but not expecting me either. For immediately her hands went up and untied that knot of hair, letting it fall across her shoulders. Then her hands brushed her sleeves down on her arms, and dusted off her blouse.

"Thank you," I said to her, and waved my hand at my clothes drying in the Sicilian sun.

She just laughed, and then said, "It was better than riding along with you smelling like Joan d'Arc." I went over and sat next to her in the sunlight, with her blanket wrapped around me, "We go down into Novara at nightfall," she said. Then she rested her head on my shoulder and a lock of her long hair draped across my chest.

"What was the name of that village where you grew up?"

"I didn't grow up there," she said, and pushed the hair back out of her face, without lifting her head from my shoulder. "I spent the summers there, some years, when my father was too busy in the courts."

"But what is it called?"

"Castellnotte."

"Will you take me there?"

She sat up, drawing her legs up and wrapping her arms around them in a hug. With a toss of her head, the long hair fell down past the middle of her back. "Soon," she said. "Next, after Novara, then Tortorici, Randazzo. Then we'll come there."

"Will your father still be there? I would like to meet him."

She sat up straight, her head erect on her long neck, a frown of disbelief on her face. There was a long silence, while we both began to figure many things out. "You already know him," she said.

"I do?"

"My father is the man you call Sole. Lombardo Crisianna."

"Sole?" I said.

She nodded.

"The Sole who sent you off with Pilo's letter?"

"Rubiolo's letter," she corrected me, and reminding me that we needed to use their underground names, even though she had just revealed her father's name to me.

"But you were sitting by him at . . ." I stopped there, in order not to embarrass myself any further.

Rafaella was quiet for a moment, and then she began to laugh. "You mean you thought Father was my . . ." This time she could say no more, and she just laughed and laughed at me to fill out the rest of the words. I saw, then, that those sparkling gray eyes of hers were the same as the stark eyes in Lombardo's sharp gaze.

After a moment, I said simply, "I am happy."

Rafaella put her arms around me, her forehead on the point of my shoulder, and as she laughed her long black hair draped around me, and she hugged me tight.

"Time to go, miei ragazzi," Pilo's voice came drifting down the gully, and Rafaella and I looked up. The sound of the rushing water covered his every step. He was standing up above us in the brush, gathering up all the sun-dried clothes.

Pilo said no more than that, but in seconds Rafaella had slipped on her shoes, stood and climbed back up to the horses and to Corrao. She never looked back at me but it was not that she was embarrassed. She was simply back to the great work that lies ahead of us. I will have to wait. We will have to wait. History waits for no one.

As Pilo and I were climbing back up the hillside into the trees, he said, " I miss my Rosetta, Burtoni."

"Who is Rosetta, Count?"

"La donna mia," he said, and his steps seemed to slow and wander a bit in the volcanic gravel. "Mia carissima, Burtoni. She is back in Genova, and someday I hope to join her there, when all of this is over. When it is all accomplished, I will join her in Italia. Not in Savoia or Piedmonte or Liguria, or hiding in Switzerland again. I will join her in Italia."

Not once, in all the many weeks we've spent together now, have I ever heard Rosalino Pilo speak of anyone, let alone of anyone special, any Rosetta. So what he said now was a complete surprise. And it drew us closer together too, as comrades, as brothers.

"Someday," he said, hugging the bundle of dry and clean clothes warmed by the sun. "My Rosetta and I, we will live together, in a free land. And then maybe, my friend," he looked over at me with a warmth that was new. "Maybe you will come to visit us, Burtoni, from your Sicilian village. From your free Sicilia. With your carissima, no?" And he grinned at me with a wink. "She is a beautiful girl, Burtoni," he said, "and she has a great heart. You have chosen well."

I said something, I don't even remember now what I said exactly. I tried to laugh it off, I guess. But all the while I was remembering the hug of Rafaella's arms around my shoulders, and I dreamed of mountaintop villages above the sea. Of this place called Castellnotte, of which she speaks.

I dream and I remember it all now.

12.

16 April
Novara di Sicilia

We rode down into town last night in the dark, and we spent the few hours just before dawn posting our handwritten signs on all the walls. They are written in Sicilian by Rosalino, so I can't make most of it out. But I can make out the broad print at the top, proclaiming that the General is on his way. The General and his army.

In a little piazza below the village church, with a rise of ten stairs up to the wooden doors of this little duomo, Count Rosalino Pilo lined us up. He stood at the top of the stairs and Corrao and I stood a few steps lower, at attention. Two steps lower still, between us, we stacked five of the muskets, their bayonets fixed, and we rested them up like a haystack, the points of those new bayonets reaching for the blue Sicilian sky. And then, to finish the effect, one step beneath the muskets Pilo had us scatter a few handfuls of shot, and an open crate of grenades, to make it seem we had ammunition to waste.

Pilo was wearing his saber in its scabbard, his long hair swept back on his shoulders, and with the façade of the church behind us, and all of these weapons at his feet, with Corrao and me at stern attention, he did look tall and fierce. Even if he was short and slight and pale, he stood like a prince up there looking down at the little square.

It was Rafaella's job to gather up the Novarani as they slowly awoke to their day. She wandered around the square, and into some of the side streets, and she knocked on doors and windows. She pointed at the hand-lettered bills we'd posted in the dark. There may have been some scowls and grumbling at first, but I must admit, one look into Rafaella's sweet face, and all the grumbling stopped. It is partly her beauty, but it is also the intensity and the truth in her eyes. I know that I will follow her where ever she leads. But this magic of hers seems to hold many others under its spell.

Once there were a dozen or so people gathered before the steps, Pilo began to speak. He used Sicilian, and for these people this means everything. Their guttural, clipped language with its softening 'oo's' to rhyme the words reaches deep into their hearts in ways I can only guess at, and it means I can only guess at exactly what Count Pilo was saying. But I could hear enough to know that he was promising them the General. Il Generale is coming, with an army of thousands, and if they stand forth now, their land will be free. They will be free.

While Pilo was speaking, a thin short priest poked his head out of the church. The look on his face said simply, 'Who is stirring up trouble, here on the church steps, when my people should be coming to mass.' But then he seemed to listen, and I saw real fear in his eyes, and he just as quietly disappeared back inside his church. If Rosalino Pilo even saw him, he never let on.

The crowd was silent though. They listened carefully, and never even spoke among themselves. After about half an hour, Pilo said to Corrao and me, "Collect the muskets, boys. Let's go."

It seemed to me we had failed. Pilo walked down into his little congregation, and there was then a lot of whispered and urgent conversation. Some of the Novarani wandered up the stairs past us and went into the church, though mostly they were the women. Giovanni and I gathered up the arms and the open crate, and then carefully collected the artfully strewn ammunition, every priceless piece of it, and carried it all off to the horses we'd ridden in on. Rafaella had disappeared somewhere.

When we came back, the piazza was nearly empty, along with all my hopes, and I noticed, glancing around the square, that every one of our handbills was gone. They had vanished into someone's hands. Completely stripped away, like some hidden shame. 'And this is where we came to begin the revolution,' I thought.

After that, Rafaella led us down one of the streets, I won't record here which one and I won't now write down any names. It is too dangerous, I realize now, in a town like this, if this journal should fall into the wrong hands, into the hands of someone we can't trust. Spies are everywhere. I must always remind myself of this.

So we walked down the narrow street and Rafaella led us to some friends of hers who quietly fed us and showed us to a few beds where we could rest in the warm afternoon. There was only one strange thing, and this I will put down. The priest came later, and he ate with us and he blessed our food. I don't know what this means, or whose side he is on, but I am suspicious. To many of these men wearing collars can't be trusted. And he may be one of them.

So it has been a long journey, and a long ride to get here, only to find this failure. Only to hide in some stranger's house, and eat with the town priest. The Novarani, with their fear and their paralysis, their lack of will and courage. It all makes me think of the General on his island, and I understand now why he wants to stay there. Why he waits.

But as we try to sleep out of the afternoon sun, Rosalino Pilo is writing letters again, to leave here to be posted. One of them, I see, is long and written to his Rosetta. But the other, it is very brief. It just tells lies to the General, I'm sure. Lies that will lead him into war. Our war. Our imagined war.

If it weren't that I found Rafaella here, I fear all would be lost. Today, everything is a waste. Except there is now for me Rafaella.

13.

17 April
near Tortorici

Our ride was long, all through the night on rugged mountain trails, then in the morning we entered the next village, Tortorici, it was called. Rafaella leads us to the towns we need to reach, the towns ready to head our call. And today there are ten of us.

You see, yesterday I was wrong. Because there was no shouting, no marching in the streets, no taking up arms and waving them in the air, because the Novarani were so quiet and calm as they listened to Count Pilo speak, so I thought all was lost. But Rafaella Crisiana was right, after all.

We got up late after night had fallen, ate a heavy pasta soaked in oil with a plain red wine, took the bread and olives and fruit they gave us, and the four of us rode out of town. At the edge of the village seven men met us. Six of them were on horseback, and the little priest was there on foot. Four of the Novarani brought muskets with them, the fifth hand an old cutlass, and the sixth one called Gaetano was carrying just a hatchet in his hands. But they all to a man came armed.

Then the priest blessed us, for whatever that is worth. But I still don't trust him, or his kind. I've seen too many of them now, to trust any of them from the first, though they seem different down here in the South, in Sicily.

And yet, now we are ten, and we are gazing down in the first morning light on the next little town Rafaella has found for us. She seems to know just where we should go. And Count Pilo, he's not really grinning, but he sits astride that horse like a proud general, now, his hair streaming back in the breeze like a lion, because he is making his lies come true.

14.

20 April
Randazzo

Too busy now to write. We have ridden hard these last days, and the Nebrodi are hard, rugged mountains to cross, and harder still to cross in the dark. There are so many streams with torrents running fast and full of the late spring waters, and it would be easy with a slip or a fall to lose a horse along here. Rafaella directs us, but she no longer leads the way. It is too dangerous in the dark. One of the local men always leads the way now, sometimes on foot, and they wind us through the oak and maple groves and around the streams where we would most certainly be lost without them. We stop each morning at a different town, and as it was with the Novarani, each evening we leave with more men. Alcara Li Fosi. Cesaro. Today Randazzo.

We are now twenty-five strong. So when this morning we lined up in front of the little duomo, there are few weapons to stack up on the stairs. Instead now there are columns of men, rag tag but fierce, and now there are shouts and cheers when Pilo speaks. No more the worried silences. No more the furrowed brows and closed mouths. No more the furtive glances around the piazza. Our numbers have loosed our tongues.

I understand too how it all works. Each morning, as we arrive in a village, Rafaella moves about in the soft dawn light and posts our broadsides on the walls of the main piazza. This is so that the awakening contadini understand, when they see us armed and arranged before their church. Those who can read pass the word quickly. We are not a band of brigands, though this must certainly be what we look like. And we are not the hated Neapolitans, not the Bourbon horde. We have not come to take or to demand or to steal. We have come to ask for their help, for help on the pathways to their own freedom.

So then Count Pilo makes his speech, with his growing squadron at his feet, and at the end we brandish our arms, and we all shout, "Viva Sicilia!" and "Liberta!"

And yes, we are now a squadron, and soon perhaps we will even be a brigade. We grow and grow with each passing day.

After the last shout of "Liberta!" the men break up to be fed and to sleep, for still we travel only at night. But now we don't need to demand or even ask for supplies, for at every village the people take us in. We are fed, simply but well, and our animals are cared for.

And while we are resting, Rafaella walks back to the piazza and carefully takes down each one of those posted sheets, rolls them up and packs them away. Remember, they are handwritten, by Count Rosalino himself.   It was Rafaella and Rosalino made them together, back in the hills above Messina before we set out.   Written in proper Sicilian, they aren't being torn down or hidden, as I thought they were.   No, they are too valuable to be wasted.   So she gathers them all back up, and tucks them safely away until the next village is in oursight.

Tomorrow, I believe, we reach Castellnotte. It is Rafaella's old home.   And it is half the way to Palermo, or close to that.

Again Rosalino Pilo writes a letter, to be left and posted to the General, as we make our way on toward the capitol.   Corrao often laughs at him, making fun of Pilo's little tre colore lies.   But that is just Corrao's way.   In truth, he likes a lie, especially when it works.

15.

23 April
near Mistrette

The squadron has grown to over fifty now.   It is becoming hard to keep track of us all, and harder still to feed us when we descend upon the next little village.   It takes all their resources, and more.   Still we never need to ask for food or for places to sleep. But everyone who joins us now must bring his own weapon, and this has begun to be a problem. The people here are poor, too poor to give up the one gun they have in a household that needs it to hunt for their sustenance. It is too great a sacrifice, too precious a tool, to irreplaceable to lose.   But still they keep joining us. Even if they are barehanded, they come.   They swear, some of them, they will fight with bare fists.   They follow us, more and more of them, each night. More.

16.

24 April

The little village of Castellnotte sits on a high hillside and gazes down from those heights to the sea. If you walk out from the Chiesa Santa Lucia and its little piazza you come to a short stone wall, perhaps 2 feet high, and from there descends a staircase about ten feet wide, switching back and forth down the rock face, it leads down the steep rock walls to the shore.

When everything was quiet, in the sleepy afternoon, Rafaella took my hand and said, "I want you to see something, my Burtoni."   And so she led me down those stairs in the white, sea light, all the way down to the rocky shoreline, a hundred long steps or more, back and forth on the switches.   And all along the way down, she kept pointing at islands far out in the sea. "Watch how they disappear, how the horizon rises as we come down," she said, and she kept a firm hold on my hand.

I thought that the turquoise blue water and creamy white peaks of its waves on the rose gray stones of the shoreline were what she wanted to show me, or maybe it was something about those disappearing islands out on the ocean that was her point, for we nearly ran down the stairs, and all the way she kept her tight grip on my hand. But I was wrong, for the very moment we reached the waterline, she wrapped her arms around me and turned me back toward the village above, and in that shining light I saw what she wanted me to see.

You see, every single one of those hundred and more steps was trimmed around its entire edge with small ceramic tiles. As I gazed up from the rocky beach, I saw a pathway that ascended from the seashore up to the face of the church, and each and every step glistened with the blue of the Mediterranean and the yellow of the lemons and a especially with a startlingly pure white of their hearts. Here and there you see splashes and hints of the red a royal cardinal wears. But all of it is surrounded in their pure shining white.

"It's beautiful, isn't it?" Rafaella said.

She still held me tight, and my arms were wrapped in the strength of her hug, so that I couldn't hold her the way I wanted to embrace her. The stairs led my eyes up with all their colors until they reached to the graceful arch of the portico of Santa Lucia, and from this distance it was as blue as the clear Sicilian sky, and glowing white with touches of orange and red. It, too, is one great ceramic tile, all of them painted by hand by the artists of Castellnotte. High above the church, framing it all, stood the gray stone fortification of La Rocca. There lay the castle where the English duke and his family lived. And all of this, together, is beautiful Castellnotte.

Suddenly Rafaella kissed me on the cheek and let me go. Then she took my hand and began leading me back up the stairs, but now we stopped for a moment at almost every step to admire the paintings on the tiles. I could see that each step took a different subject, and every little six-inch square of majolica was carefully painted. There was a step of tulips in red and yellows and oranges, with lime green stems. There was a step of blue green fish, and the next above a step of decorated fishing boats, all of them in a rainbow of shades. There was a step of red purple grapes, and one of lemons, and one of little tangerines and blood red oranges like Rafaella had eaten the night we met.

"This is one of my favorites," she said, and sat down on the stair with her legs curled up alongside her so I could see. "These are the fishermen, see all their brown faces."

It is surprising how, as I gazed down the stairway, they seem just plain and normal stones from above. All of the majolica is hidden from your eyes when you look down except for an occasional hint of color, like a tiny wildflower in a crack. But once you turn and look up, toward the village, toward the church of Santa Lucia, it all becomes a riot of crazy hues framed in sharp, stark white.

Behind Rafaella, on the step above the fishermen, the row of tiles were all tiny women's faces, with bright smiling red lips and almond eyes feathered with black lashes like waves. I sat down on the step next to her, and a horrible awkward silence fell over both of us. I took her hands in mine and I gazed in her eyes, as sweet and almond-shaped as the faces surrounding her on the tiles. But then I glanced away, and my heart was pounding again, and my mind was empty of words, as dry as my mouth. Here I was, having chased the women of Montevideo and Nizza and Genova around and around, and with at least a bit of success. But now I was as dumb and speechless as a boy.

"What is it?" she said, with her red smiling lips and her dark black eyes. And she said, "What do you want to say? Burtoni?"

I stared out at the sea to try to find some of the words that were singing in my heart, filled with confusion and fears, not just the blood and passion of my years, but then she simply whispered the words that I was searching for. "Burtoni," Rafaella said. "I am yours."

She gazed fearlessly into me, with the same courage that has led this whole squadron here to Castellnotte. "You know that, don't you?" she said.

I nodded yes, but still I was mute and stupid. She smiled at me, and then she laughed and tossed her head so her long hair furled back and her lips parted, and she was more beautiful than all the tiny painted beauties surrounding her on the stair. Then she said, "Burtoni? Don't you have something to say to me?"

My face grew hot and my stupid tongue was still parched and dead. Then somehow, I blurted out, "My heart is yours alone, Rafaella." Then without thinking, I added, "Forever."

How can I tell her what that means? How do I explain to her my strange affliction? Why? Why did I say that word? For me, "Forever" is so very long a time. I can't even say how long a time, for I don't know. How dare I speak that word, ever? How dare I? I am a freak. I have no right to speak to her in such a way.   Forever? The damnation of Forever.

But Rafaella does not notice my turmoil, or she takes it to be just bashfulness. So she leaned forward, and she took my silly face in her two hands and kissed me on the lips. And then, before I could really respond, she leapt up and scurried ahead of me up the stairs. Two at a time she leapt over them, the sunflowers and the sailing ships, the olive trees and the shepherdesses, the angels and the mariners, and so many more above us on our path.

She never stopped running until she reached the piazza above. She didn't pause to gaze down at another stair, until I caught her finally, both of us laughing, right at the door of the church. I wrapped my arms around her then, and held her tight, and she seemed so tiny in my embrace.

"Someday," I said to her, "When all this is over . . ."

But Rafaella's gaze drew my eyes up to the large majolica in the façade crowning the church door. It held a pale sky blue, ten feet across, and the dark haired figure of the Saint stood there alone, with wafts of brown and green Sicilian landscape behind her. It was the image of that Saint that made me quiet.

She was beautiful, dressed in billowing rose and white, her hair black and flowing around the almond of her face, with startlingly blue eyes gazing gently down at us, all sinners at her feet. Her hands were folded peacefully in prayer, and like this little village, she seemed quiet and distant from every trouble, and lovely almost beyond compare.

But there in the crease of her neck, beneath her placid, restful face, beneath her benevolent gaze, a dagger was thrust into the martyr's neck, and from it a medallion of ruby red blood dripped down onto her breast, frightening in that bare brilliant red surrounded by a world that seemed made of peaceful rose and heaven blue and purest white. This image was so startling that my words, right as I spoke, drifted off into meaninglessness. I couldn't finish this thought of 'someday.' Someday. We both fell silent, though I realized then that Rafaella had brought me here to see just that, to see this troubling Saint. "Who is she?" I said, after a moment.

"Santa Lucia," she said. And then, "Isn't she beautiful?"

Before I could answer in any way, Rafaella grabbed my hands again and, like a child, she cried, "Come on! I want you to meet the Duke." And so we began to run again up out of the piazza toward La Rocca, the barren castle standing above is. "Oh, and the Duchess too," she said, a laughing afterthought.

Rosalino Pilo has paused here in the mountains near Mistrette, because our force of men needs to get organized. There are so many of us now, he has divided our squadron into two. He leads one, and Captain Corrao the other. So yes, he is Captain Giovanni Corrao now.

Perhaps Rosalino could have made us into three squadrons, and given me a lead. But I think that my apparent youth deceives him. He thinks I'm just a boy, a wild lad, which means he hasn't stopped to count all the years that led him to me. He is not thinking about Anzani, or the flight from Morrazone. If he did, he would know that my looks betray me. I am no boy. And if he can count, he would know that. But Rosalino Pilo in the end, I guess, doesn't care. My looks deceive him. And two squadrons we are.

But then, I did disappear yesterday with Rafaella, for the whole afternoon and we did not report back to Captain Pilo until this morning. So perhaps that is it. Rosalino only smiled at me, when I reported back in the morning. He gave me that look, just like he did when he was talking about his Rosetta back in the hills above Novara.

And maybe he is right. Maybe I am too in love, too head over heels, to be trusted to lead a squadron into war. Recklessness in love does not lead to wisdom in battle. He knows this, as do I. "Burtoni, you take care of the horses for me, lad, and then just be sure your musket is clean," he ordered. And then he said, "Corrao and I will be drilling these new recruits all afternoon. We've got to make some real soldiers out of them, before we reach Palermo. And before the General arrives."

Before I could ask, 'Have you heard? Is he coming?' Count Pilo grinned and ordered, "After you are done, take the afternoon off. Go find your girl, lad. Go on. Time is short."

But my Rafaella is busy doing something for the Duchess. And that is why I have time now to write this all down here, in all this great detail. I have time to think alone now, and to prepare for the battle ahead. If I choose.

Lord Burmonte, the Duke of Castellnotte, opened the door himself. He is a tall, lean man with a military bearing, clean-shaven and with his steely grey hair close cropped. He seemed a bit distracted, preoccupied with some worrisome business, until his gaze passed over me and lighted on Rafaella Crisiana. Then his mouth dropped open before it spread into a broad, winning smile.

"My girl," he said in amazement, and Rafaella nearly leapt into his open armed embrace. Then he held her by the shoulders and gazed at her at arm's length, smiling and shaking his head now in disbelief. He didn't know what to say, but he seemed to know enough not to ask questions about what brought her here. "And who is this?" he asked her, smiling now at me, and offering a firm handshake. His Italian was awkward and formal, but accurate.

"Jack Burton," Rafaella said my name, in that way of hers that makes it sound so foreign. Then she said, grinning widely at me before she spoke, "Mio fidanzato."

"Ahh!" said the old Duke, his eyebrows arching up. "Welcome to Castellnotte, Jack Burton," he said all in flat, plain English.

I was still taken a little by surprise at Rafaella's announcement, but I shook the Duke's hand and managed to say, in Italian, "Here they call me Burtoni, sir."

"Burtoni," the Duke said. "Burtoni it is. Come in, my boy. Come in." Rafaella was already through the doorway.

"I must call Lady Eleanor," the Duke said. "She will be so surprised to see you, dear Rafaella, and to hear your news. Gaetano?" he called out.

A Sicilian boy, in his early teens, scurried out from inside wearing an outrageously stiff and ill-fitting suit. "Gaetano, tell the Duchess we have some surprise guests."

The Duke wheeled around to look at us again, as Gaetano disappeared somewhere back into the rooms of the castle. "Mia carina," he said smiling, his head dropping a little to lean toward her. "And her caro fidanzato. You have grown up so quickly, carina!"

Lady Eleanor Burmonte, the Duchess of Castellnotte, met us in a grand room, with frescoed ceilings twelve feet high and an eight-foot fireplace with a decorated mantle that reached nearly to that ceiling. She is shorter and rounder that the Duke, but just as gray. Like the Duke, there is an orderliness about her and she stands straight and stiff, which didn't keep the room from dwarfing her. She seemed both more surprised and less delighted to see us than the Duke. "Why, little Rafaella Crisiana, what brings you back to Castellnotte? How is your dear father Lombardo? What is he up to these days?"

We were still very careful to keep our secrets, so we didn't answer any of her questions. The Duke leapt however straight into the opening our silence left without a second thought. "And this, Eleanor," he said with an arm out toward me, speaking in English again, "is Jack Burton."

"Really," said the Duchess.

I stepped forward, awkwardly, and stuck out my hand to shake hers. But the Duchess just moved her hand toward me, hanging from a limp wrist, and too high in the air to shake. Rafaella started to giggle at this awkward moment, me with my paw stuck out frankly toward her and Lady Eleanor with her dangling hand in my face, and then at long last I realized I was supposed to kiss her hand. Since I've always spent most of my time around the docks or in the army, this is something I've never done before, and trust me, it was tough for me not to chuckle at myself when I heard Rafaella's giggles.

But the Duke, he is a clever old dog, and perceptive as a ship's cat. He swooped over in one move and had one arm around my shoulder and the other around the Duchess. "Signor Burtoni, Eleanor, is our Rafaella's intended."

"Really," said the Duchess again. And as her arm dropped to her side, she took a new look at me, as if to appraise the property more carefully. Then she looked over again at Rafaella and smiled. Remember, we have been living on horseback in these same clothes for better than a week since Rafaella washed out the remains of Jean d'Arc from them. And Rafaella is in trousers nearly the same as mine, and nothing even near to a dress, certainly no dress like the Duchess was wearing, with lace edging that brushes against the spotless marble floors. But I guess from the way she reacted, the Duchess like the Duke had seen Rafaella in pants before.

"Congratulations, Rafaella," the Duchess said. "And you too, Mister Burton."

"Burtoni is fine, ma'am," I said at the same time as the Duke said, "Signor Burtoni, Eleanor."

And so we all laughed, and it lightened the air in general, at least as much as I can ever expect from this Duchess of Castellnotte, I suspect.

Then the Duchess nodded her head curtly at me, and said, in Italian finally, "Signor Burtoni, can you and your fidanzata stay to dinner?"

I was still getting used to hearing that word, and I had to stop myself from asking like a fool, 'Who?' And it was all so confusing, and in too many languages. I fell back into my American English, of a sort. "Yup," I said, sounding like a peasant to these British ears.

That made us all laugh again.

It may have been a poor countryside, but you'd never know it by that table the Duke and Duchess placed before us. The evening started with platters of olives and crusty bread from a wood-fired oven, along with a white buttery cheese coated with fennel seeds and covered with the pale green olive oil from the estate of Castellnotte. We drank fruity white wine along with this, and the Duchess busily directed "the staff" from her end of the long table, while the Duke proudly described the olives and the oil and what parts of his estate they came from.

I thought this would be the whole meal, so I dug in heartily. I really couldn't conceive of what was to come. Not after weeks of sea voyaging and horseback travel through backcountry, I couldn't.

Gaetano led the way, but there must have been a dozen or more young ladies and lads who waited on us, bringing in the food in shifts and then sweeping away our dirty plates, and always filling our wine glasses. Next they brought out small plates with tagliatelle in the same oil, coated like a snowfall with some white salty cheese. Then came a glass of a hardy simple red wine, and that was still only for starters. For the main meal, at last, slices of duck breast arrived in a sauce of sweet orange and vinegar. And remember, this was all unplanned. Rafaella had just dropped in out of the heavens on them.

While we were eating the tagliatelle, the Duchess called Gaetano over to her place at the table, and whispered but one word to him. "Spada," she said quietly, so neither the Duke nor Rafaella heard, as they were talking. And so then out came another small side plate, with grilled slices of eggplant, and on each plate there was a thin slice of swordfish, rolled with eggplant and ham and grilled through, the whole of it drizzled in the rich oil flecked with green bits of olive.

Rafaella squealed with delight and laughed out loud when she saw the swordfish arrive. "Involtini!" she squealed. And that made the Duchess laugh too, smiling fondly at her.

"This was our little Rafaella's favorite," the Duke explained to me. "When she lived here at Castellnotte."

The wine was going a bit to my head by now, I have to admit. I have never in all my years eaten like this, and we were far from done. The children brought out tumblers of cool spring water then and little platters with thinly sliced fennel sprinkled with raisins and drizzled again with that rich oil. As we nibbled on it with our fingers, I realized it was meant to clear away the heavy taste of the duck and the richness of the buttery swordfish. For at the end, out came little cakes seasoned with fennel seeds and orange and accompanied with a tiny stemmed glass of a brown, bittersweet liquor scented with almonds.

By this point, I was as full as I've ever been, and my head was spinning with all the wine and liquor. A grand sense of contentment billowed up from deep in my heart, and I understood at the end of this magical day what it is about Castellnotte that makes it all so enchanting to Rafaella. Castellnotte is not part of our everyday world. No, it is alone, and separate, and it is magic, indeed. It is a land of dreams.

Almost all of our talk at the table was about the food, and the Duke in particular revelled in describing the delicacies of each course. But Rafaella too kept telling me about where this wine or that eggplant and these sweet fennel bulbs came from all around Castellnotte. During that long, wondrous meal, there was only once a sour moment. While we were eating the rich duck breast, Rafaella held up her glass of red wine and said, "My father planted these grapes before I was born."

"Long before you were born, my dear one," the Duke of Brumonte said, with a warm smile. "It was Lombardo and your Grandfather Rafaello who put them in the ground, back when Lombardo was just a wee little lad. Long before Eleanor and I came to Castellnotte. But here we sit, enjoying the fruits of old Rafaello's artistry and his labor, with you my carina Rafaella, his granddaughter. "

"And our granddaughter too," the Duchess added, along with her own sweet smile.

"Grandfather loved these grapes," Rafaella said.

Then the Duchess spoke from her end of the table, and a sudden frigidness that was peculiar came over her. "And how is Lombardo?" she asked one more time. " We haven't heard from him for a long, long while now."

There was an awkward moment of silence, and the Duke glanced at me as the Duchess's and Rafaella's eyes met across the loaded table. "He is well," Rafaella answered, not saying much at all.

"And his law practice there," The Duke leapt in to ward off anymore of the awkward silences, "it is doing well too?"

"Well" said the Duchess, ignoring her husband's question, "we do miss Lombardo here. This place was never so well run as when he ran it."

"That was years ago," Rafaella said, sounding as cool now as the Duchess.

"Nearly twenty years ago," the Duchess added precisely.

"He was most remarkable at managing this estate, I must say," the Duke nodded along. "We took it over, you know, Signor Burtoni, not long after his father died. And the two of them, Rafaello and Lombardo, they had built up Castellnotte to what we are enjoying tonight. Without Lombardo and his father Rafaello this place would be just a run down mess. But they made it into an estate."

"And what is he doing now in Messina?" the Duchess interrupted.

Rafaella glanced at me as if to remind me to keep still, but I didn't need to be reminded, and she saw that immediately. "He has his law practice," she answered the Duchess vaguely, but stared at me the whole while.

"And is he still mixed up with these country ruffians and their revolutions?" the Duchess asked.

That was when the real, heavy silence fell across the table. Rafaella turned an iron gaze on the Duchess, and didn't answer. I sat there awkwardly for a moment, and I felt my temper rising. These English nobles with their high ways were not about to insult my Rafaella. So it was going to be difficult for me to keep my mouth shut.

The Duke, whose glance flitted back and forth among the three of us, appraising each one of us, calmly changed the subject. "So, have you chosen a day for the wedding, carina?"

At that, Rafaella let a smile drift slowly onto her lips, a miracle it was, and she followed the Duke's lead. Grinning, she looked over at me across the table and said, "Sort of. But not exactly."

"And what does that mean?" the Duke of Brumonte laughed.

Both Rafaella and I were remembering my pledge on the majolica stairs: 'Someday, when all of this is over . . .'

"It means we know when," I said as I smiled back at her, at my fidanzata, "so we don't really have a date yet."

I said those words without fear or worry, with only a great lightness in my heart. Maybe it was easy because there was no date to be set. And maybe I had no date to be set. And maybe I had no fears because there is so much to be afraid of between now and that someday. It is easier to imagine myself winding up hanging from some Bourbon gallows, or lingering away on some desert island prison built of the hardest stone, than it is to imagine that 'someday' we spoke of, no, that 'someday 'we both dream of.

Yet I don't think that is it. You see, a deep commitment has lodged down in my heart and I have found a partner for my soul in this tangled, ugly world. With her I will fly always, but never away. She is too filled with courage. And so these words are easy and fearless for me. They arise in my heart gently and with boundless joy.

*　　　　*　　　　*

The iciness of that moment passed quickly, and we did not speak again of Lombardo or of rebellions. The Duke and the Duchess never asked how we had come there or where we were headed. As if in silent agreement, those questions never arose, and Rafaella and I never spoke of them before Lord Brumonte and Lady Eleanor.

Suddenly, the Duchess sat up straight and over that strong almond liquor, she suddenly proposed, "Would you like to have the wedding here, child?"

The Duke sprang to life at those words as well. "What a wonderful idea!" he exclaimed. "It would be such a celebration, and Eleanor and I would just love to help get you two launched properly. The way you deserve, mia carina."

I could see that Rafaella like the idea, her gray eyes brightened to a soft sea green, but she looked over at me and paused. At that moment, I assumed she was looking at me for approval, and how could I turn her down. Especially with my head full of wine, capped off by that sneaky sweet liquor.

"I think this is a fine idea," I spouted up, letting all the grapes talk.

But the moment I spoke out, my Rafaella looked down at the table, and she surprised me again. "I suppose we could," she said, without looking up at any of us.

"Oh, it would be wonderful, " the Duke slapped his hands together, and then rubbed them happily as if he were ready to get to work.

And the Duchess, I thought for a moment she was going to jump up and call to the servants and commence with the decorating right then and there. "You know, Rafaella, the giardino d'arancia in the courtyard would be perfect, especially in the spring when the fruit is so full. But next fall too, when they begin to blossom. Then it would be perfect for a wedding."

Rafaella raised her head at the mention of this garden. "The orange grove," she whispered toward me, and then gazing in my eyes, she said, "I suppose we could, if it is what you want."

"If it is what you want," I said, and reached across the corner of the table to take her hand.

"If it is what you both would like," said the Duke. And then he added, "Wonderful."

And he made us all laugh at that.

I spent that night sleeping in a billowy soft feather bed, softer than any bed I've ever known. The Duke winked at me, and then he and the Duchess swept Rafaella away safely, deep within the complicated, stone hallways of La Rocca. It took a long while for me to fall asleep that night, my excitement was jumbled and confused by all I have seen and heard and learned on this amazing day, this miraculous day that has changed the whole of my life. An old jaded cuss like me, swept away by the drink and by the twinkle in a young girl's eye. But in the end the wine and the twinkle did their trick, and my head drifted away without any protest down into the deep, fluffy pillows.

Still it was early, before first light, when I awoke, still a bit groggy and not really rested, but now unable to sleep. The effects of all the alcohol had worn away and left me tired but awake and sleepless. I listened as the birds awakened and began to sing. And then I realized it was time for us to leave this dreamy, easy existence. Count Rosalino Pilo and his two squadrons were awaiting us, waiting to press on toward Palermo. And they would need Rafaella and me to arouse the sleeping giant of Caprera. So it was time to leave the lantern lights and the long full tables and the shining majolica colors of Castellnotte.

She arrived at my door as the early light poured in the windows. Rafaella was dressed again for the road, just as I was. The dust of the Nebrodi foothills was on our boots. The call of our duty has returned, like the worn off wine, and we made ready to depart. It was clear to me, though I'm not sure why, that Rafaella wanted to slip away before the Duke and Duchess awoke.

She led me silently down a back hallway and downstairs through the servants' quarters. Already the children who work in the castle were up and moving about, quietly working in the depths of La Rocca.

Rafaella put one finger to her lips to keep me silent, and then she opened a dark green wooden shutter so I could look out onto the courtyard. She didn't need to explain what it was that she was showing me, or why she wanted me to see it. Slabs of pink streaked marble cut into a octagons and then fit into a pattern that radiated out like sunlight from the center and stretched under the arches around the little courtyard. Each stone was edged with a lively green border of something as old and mossy as the castle. Dead center in the courtyard stood a short ancient tree, surrounded with a stone hexagonal bench that echoed the shapes of the flooring stones. And all around the periphery of the courtyard were similar old dwarf trees, maybe at most ten feet high. Eight of them, like the eight sides to the cut pieces of marble. And they were all filled with round bright oranges, and here and there the fruit had ripened and fallen onto the marble stones. Tiny birds were flitting about and just beginning to sing in the early light. This, I know in my heart in a moment, is the giardino d'arancia.

I smiled and nodded my head to show her that I understood and approved. This little orchard will be a wonderful place to be married, to be joined forever. And I didn't allow myself to think about what forever meant.

That was when Gaetano appeared, and he led us down more stairs and out into the stables, where two fresh horses awaited us. Not the Jean d'Arc and the old nag we had ridden to Castellnotte. Gaetano took my hand, and he held my shoulder in his other hand and said in a whisper, "I would join you. But I must feed my mother and my two little sisters. So for now, my friends, only my heart goes out from here with you. Take my courage at your side, sir."

Then he gave Rafaella a hard long hug, the embrace of a deep old familial love. I understood from that embrace that they had worked together here, when Gaetano must have been just a child. I noticed then that a younger boy and two girls stood back in the shadows of the stable. We mounted up on these fine fresh horses, and then Gaetano said, "When the time comes, we will be with you." And he gave my horse a gentle slap. The other young servants opened a gate for us and out we rode into the gentle morning light.

Rafaella led us down out of the village and then up into the high hills where the squadrons of Pilo were waiting. When we were out of sight of the castle, I called out to her and for a moment we slowed our horses to a walk.

"It is beautiful," I said to her, "Castellnotte."

She just smiled and nodded in agreement.

"But, Rafaella, why did you hesitate? Isn't that orange grove where we should be married?"

She looked away at the woods, the same way she had looked down at the table last night, when the Duchess proposed the garden. A sudden shadow passed over us, and then she said without ever looking back at me, "Yes, Castellnotte is where we should be married." She paused and then looked at me again. "That garden would be wonderful."

I rode on a few more steps at a canter. Then I pulled my horse up to a stop. "What's wrong, Rafaella. What's bothering you, that you won't say?"

She let her horse step loosely over some stones, and she said then looking directly at me, "I don't know, Jack Burton, if my father will ever return here." At that, she gave the spur to her horse and I followed her off across the hillsides at a gallop, searching for the fires of the squadrons of the Count.

Giovanni Corrao met me with a scowl and a long silence when we returned. He looked Rafaella and me both over slowly, and then said only, "Fine horses." He turned and walked away.

Rosalino though, he was different. When I reported to him, hurrying to his side while Rafaella took care of the horses, Pilo was sitting on a large stone, pen in hand, writing another missive to the General, or another announcement that the General had arrived, I'm not sure which. He looked up at me, and a broad grin spread across his face. I expected him to say my name, from the way he looked up, and then follow that with a happy halloo. And then I was prepared to get on with it, to ask for my orders, under whose command I would serve. These were the words I prepared in my head, and I was ready to stand and serve them up. But Pilo stunned me with what he said.

He let out a little chuckle to accompany that broad smile of his, and then he said, nodding his head sagely, "That Rafaella, lad, she must be some kind of woman!"

17.

6 May
Piani dei Greci

We have reached the hills above the Conca d'Oro, and at night we look down now on the lights of Palermo. I have not written for days, for there are now more than 150 of us. Men are coming from the countryside and from the villages we've never even been near, for the word is out now. Everyone who arrives has heard, the General is coming. The revolt is not over, it has only just begun. "Piddu," they call him in their dialect here. Piddu will be landing soon, they say, bringing thousands of men from the north.

So now, you see, it is taking all our time, Pilo and Corrao and I, to try to keep some sort of order here. Some of these men, like the dozen picciotti from Corleone who arrived three days ago, they are already in gangs, already organized with leaders of their own, and these boys take even more watching. For they could get an idea in mind, and one of these gangs might run off and start some attack too soon, before we are ready. Wild as these hills they live in, they are.

It is easy to see why the revolts here have failed so many times in the past. There is a deep disorder here, and a fundamental distrust of everyone but your blood family. And even there, the disruption seems to be lurking just under the surface. But at the same time, there are generations and generations of rebellion and dissent here, and their hunger to throw off the oppressor is true and deep and firm. Amongst themselves at night by the fires they speak of the Normans, not these Bourbons who rule from Napoli. And they sing songs about the revolt of "I Vesperi" some 600 years ago. I can see it too in their stone faces, in the way they look at me as a stranger and wonder silently why I am here. Rebellion is deep down in their bones. As deep as their distrust.

But "Piddu" they trust. I don't know why, but their "Piddu" they trust, even though he comes from the north. Even though they've never seen him before, and wouldn't know him now if he strolled into our camps right now. But Piddu they trust.

18.

12 May
Piani die Greci

It has come true. Pilo's plan has worked.

We now count ourselves in the hundreds, and every day more picciotti pour into this camp that has become a village almost overnight. They come in gangs now, and they are loosely organized and everyone is armed with something, some hunting musket or an old pistol. I can tell that Corrao is excited by them, their billowing spirit charges him like horse under hard rein.

This morning just after dawn a rider arrived from the west coast. His winded horse came into the camp, he fell from the saddle and asked for Rubiolo. Because he had one of Pilo's many secret names on his lips, we brought him straight away to the Count.

I was awakened by the cheers and shouts rolling through the camp. "Piddu," they called and some other things in their language I couldn't understand. Rafaella was lying beside me, when they brought this boy into Rosalino. The men around him were practically holding him up.

"Rubiolo?" the boy said to Count Pilo, who was standing now in the tent. Pilo just nodded a curt and regal yes. At moments of quiet command like this, the nobility of his roots showed in his every move.

Then the boy spoke, the words of his dialect spilling out quickly, and all around him men began to shout and wave their guns in the air.

"He has landed in Marsala, and taken the city," Rafaella whispered in my ear. I held her tightly, but none of us made a sound. We waited for Pilo's reaction, while the shouts of "Piddu" and "Marsala" echoed through the camps. The guns began to be fired in the air, foolishly wasting the precious little ammunition we had.

Rosalino Pilo was calm, without even a smile crossing his lips. He looked over for just a moment at me, and I expected him to wink. But he was too controlled for even that. He just nodded his head at me. His plan had worked, by God. The sleeping giant of Caprera was awake now, and he was on the march.

Then Pilo looked at one of the picciotti waving his handgun around in the air, and ordered him sharply, "Put that away. Get this boy some wine, and something to eat."

Then he turned to Corrao and said, "Giovanni, get out there and remind these men that they are soldiers and not boys. They should be saving their bullets for the King of Naples."

With a nod, Corrao disappeared outside quickly and before long we all heard his deep voice shouting orders, drawing these Sicilians into their squadrons. Soon the night was silent again, broken by random cheers for "Piddu" rising spontaneously from out of the earth itself and only then, so it seemed, from the men.

*   *   *

While the boy ate, Pilo sat with him drinking a glass of wine and asking him calmly question after question. For most of Rosalino's queries the lad seemed to have no answer, or at best only vague information. In the end Pilo turned from the table and said to Rafaella, "Find me a rider who knows the way to Marsala. And one who knows all the back roads and byways, Crisiana. Not just the main route."

She left my side and began asking questions in Sicilian outside. In ten or fifteen minutes, she returned with one of the picciotti, a man in his twenties, dark and short. "He knows the way," she said to Pilo.

"What is your name?" Pilo asked, speaking in Sicilian.

"Michele."

"You speak Italian, boy?" he spoke in Italian, using the familiar "tu."

"Yes," the lad said.

"So please tell me, then, where are you from, Michele," Pilo barked, still speaking in Italian, but switching now to the formal 'you.'

"Calatafimi," the boy answered.

Pilo nodded, then he sat down and dashed off a quick letter to the General, and signed his name large and florid. When he was finished, he spoke again in his most formal Tuscan. "Take this missive from us to the General," Pilo said. Handing Michele the folded paper. "When you speak to him, tell him where we are and that we await his orders, and tell him we are more than 300 ready men."

"To Piddu?" the boy's eyes glowed with his excitement.

"Yes, to il Generale himself," Rosalino went on in his Tuscan. "And to no one else. Use the back ways that you know, Michele." As he stepped away, and the lad was still standing big eyed and not moving, Pilo turned back around and speaking in Sicilian again, ordered Him. "At once, to Piddu!"

"Avanti!" the lad shouted, to show off his Italian. "Presto! Avanti!" And then he was gone at a run.

19.

16 May
Piana die Greci

Until yesterday, we heard nothing but rumors. Rosalino kept us drilling in the fields, and he had us all cleaning and oiling our weapons. The General was coming, Piddu was near, and we were all anxious. Now was the time to be truly ready. The truth is at hand.

"It will be good to see him again," I said to Rafaella one night by the fire. And not without a little pride.

"He will remember you?" she said.

"He gave me my name!" I answered, showing off to her.

"Burtoni?"

"No," I objected. "Il Rosso," I announced.

She can see through me, so easily. Rafaella just laughed at me, and called me, "John Burton," in a stiff English accent.

"Il Rosso," I said in reply. Then we both laughed.

But yesterday Michele returned with the grand news. He had ridden with Piddu up from Marsala into the interior of the island. On a rise outside his hometown the General and his thousand men had met the Bourbon army, and they had fought all day long, under the Sicilian sun. And in the end, as the darkness fell, the Bourbons had retreated from the fields of Calatafimi, back to Palermo. Piddu and the thousand had won the day. The Bourbon horde had marched out to meet them, thousands and thousands of them in the hills outside Michele's home, on the plain near Calatafimi. But the thousand in their red shirts had stood their ground, and repulsed the horde.

So now the revolution has surely begun, and with its first battles won.

Along with that news, Michele brought us orders from the General. The first we have followed already, we started immediately, tonight. The Red Shirts are coming to take Palermo, to drive the next horde of Bourbons out of the capitol. So our first task is to let the city know we are coming.

Corrao was the man who took charge, proudly. But the Count seemed to sit back and observe his friend with a smile. Corrao is the voice that speaks in Sicilian to the squadrons, but Rosalino Pilo is the leader, and the orders Corrao now speaks are coming through Pilo and from the General, from "Piddu."

Giovanni quickly gathered us into groups of 10 or 15, each little band with someone from a different local village, someone who knows the immediate area. We slipped off at dusk onto the various hillsides and then, as soon as it was dark, each band built a bonfire on a mountain promontory above the city and fanned it until it burned bright and tall.

"We will let Palermo know that the Red Shirts are coming," sang out Corrao. He raised both his arms in the air and shook his fists at the heavens. "Let them know we are here. Piddu has come!"

So it was that thirty or forty fires burned all across the mountainsides above the city. Maybe there were more, for I believe that some of the women and boys in the villages slipped off to the hills and lit signal fires too. But the mountains above Palermo tonight were speckled with light.

Corrao's orders said we should just light our fire and keep it burning until any police or guards drew near, and then we were to withdraw quickly back to the Piani. We were not to waste a shot.

Rafaella and I went out with a band led by a lad from Corleone, I'll call him Giulio after Caesar, though that is not his real name. He led us to a barren rocky bluff that gazed out over the Conca d'Oro, and we gathered wood and lit our fire. It took all ten of us to feed that blazing fire because it burned high and it burned bright all night long. And no one ever came. As sunlight broke over the edges of the sea, we abandoned the blaze to let it die down and we retreated to Piani dei Greci, following our orders.

When we returned, everyone was tired, because we'd all had the same experience. No sign of troops. No polizia. Our only fight was to keep the hungry fires burning bright the whole night long.

Tomorrow night we will return, Giulio and Rafaella and we all, we will keep the fires burning until Il Generale arrives.

20.

17 May
Piani dei Greci

Tonight there were fires down in the fringes of the city. I know that these were not our squadrons. These were the fires of the Palermitani, telling us they understand.

But one thing is different now. Those fires of the Palermitani do not last. They flare up here, and they flare up there. And always, before long, they disappear. I think the Bourbon patrols are busy dousing fires in the nighttime. And this is good, because it means that when we come, when Piddu arrives at last, they will be just as tired as we are. But more afraid.

I must write these things down. They have little or nothing to do with the great events growing all around us, I suppose, yet it was strange. I want to put down the odd talk and the funny behavior of my friend Giovanni Corrao in these hours as we wait to make history or to die. And maybe that is the explanation. Maybe Giovanni, like all of us, understands that he, that we, that none of us, may come out of the other side of this revolution alive. And so, sometimes the talk we make is strange, perhaps more important than it seems.

Yesterday morning, my Rafaella had fallen asleep while I as still awake. I find it hard sometimes, even when I am tired as the old paranza that brought us here, I can't sleep in the daylight. And so I left her sleeping and found a quiet spot under a tree and sat down to write in this journal about the lighting of the bonfires, and the fine news of the Battle of Calatafimi.

Most everyone is resting or asleep, and the field below me is scattered with men under their blankets napping or eating. From behind me somewhere, from somewhere in the rocky foothills, my friend Corrao crept up beside me. Maybe he was just trying to let everyone sleep, but he was so quiet he startled me as he sat down alongside me, and I finished the sentence I was writing and closed this book.

"Writing it all down again?" he said.

And I nodded.

"Like always," he chuckled. "Who is it for, Burtoni?"

I shrugged. "I don't know. I guess it is for whoever finds it, if . . . "

There was a moment of silence between us, broken then by Corrao's deep laugh, "If we don't make it, eh?"

"Yes, I guess that's . . ." I said.

Again there was a moment of quiet and we were looking out at the men sleeping on the warm grass below.

"Are you putting me in there, Burtoni?"

"Yes, Corrao. You are in it."

"And Rosalino?"

I nodded yes.

"Good," Corrao said. Then he reached into a little pack at his side and pulled something out. As he handed it to me, with a "here," I realized it was my red shirt, the one I'd worn in '49 when I rode with the General. The shirt Il Generale gave me, when he gave me my name.

"Where did you get that?" I said.

"From out of your stuff," he answered, and as I started to object, he raised his hand to quiet me, and said, "Burtoni, it's time for you to wear it. This is no time to be hiding it in a little bag. It will remind us to be ready, that he is coming soon." He took his hands off of the shirt and left it in my hands. "Now is the time to wear it, little Il Rosso!"

I nodded again, because he was right, and I remembered telling him during those long, still days on the quiet sea aboard The Speranza about this shirt, and my name Il Rosso, and how I came by both of them. He'd laughed at me back then, and just said, "I know at least a hundred sailors who claim that they came here with the General, and everyone of them has a red shirt to prove it. And some of those shirts even have bullet holes in them for proof. But none of them has a name to go with it. Il Rosso," he laughed. Yet he never has called me by that name. He has always called me Burtoni, and that's it.

But today, after he appeared with my shirt, filched from my pack, he seemed for the first time to believe me. To believe I'd earned that name, that it came from him, Il Generale.

"What is he like, Burtoni?" Corrao asked me, seeming weaker and more fearful than I'd ever noticed before. This was not the man with the barrel-chested laugh and the thick forearms who'd kept me from drifting overboard into the stormy sea. This was a simple man, preparing himself for coming battle, readying himself to face death and wanting to know if everything he'd heard about Il Generale was as true as he hoped. He didn't repeat the question, he just sat waiting for any answer. It took me a little while to digest what he needed to hear from me, and for the first time I believe he understood that my years and all my experience through them were older and longer than the way my young face appeared.

And so I was in no hurry. I took care to respond. "He is fair haired, and not tall, but his shoulders are broad and his strength is surprising. He is square like you, Giovanni, and plain spoken, like you too. But when he sits atop a horse, all his years in the wars on the Pampas show forth. In a saddle he is the warrior of Montevideo. And no one stands aboard a ship like he does, Corrao. No one. Giovanni, my friend, the General's sea legs are round and strong and solid. So he is always on the level, no matter how his ship is tossed."

Corrao nodded and it seemed to mean that all this he already knew. "But why do we follow him, Burtoni?" he asked. "He's lost now twice, and he's spent more time in exile than even Mazzini. Why do we keep following him?"

A grin spread across my face, I think, because I was recalling how it was to ride with him across the alps to Lugano. And I was remembering sailing the South Atlantic with him to Spain and then into Nice. "Because, Giovanni Corrao, he lifts your heart. When you are standing beside him, you know that the cause is great and that you must rise to it bravely, rise above yourself. Because, Giovanni Corrao, in his eyes we are all equal and on the road to our great freedom. And nothing will ever hold us back. Beside him, you know that is true. You don't just believe it, Giovanni, you know it."

Corrao listened quietly, soaking it all in, and then he added his own thoughts. "No, Burtoni, that's not it. Or maybe it is, but it's not all of it. I have never seen him, yet I know this much about him. He is one of us, Burtoni. He may be braver and more true of heart. He may be greater than we are. But he is one of us, still." He paused and then asked, "Isn't that true?"

While he spoke, I was pulling off my rugged shirt and then I slipped the red tunic over my head and shoulders. When I was done, I hitched my belt around my waist. "When you meet him, soon, Giovanni Corrao, you will see," I said. "Like me, you will want to follow him anywhere, because you know he is the truth."

Across the plain below us I saw Rosalino Pilo striding toward us, perhaps with some news, but perhaps not, because he seemed relaxed and happy. The Count seemed at peace, here on the verge of certain battle.

"See, Burtoni, the General is our General because," and at that moment he lowered his voice, "because he is not like that one. No, my lad," as he seemed to be fooled again by my face and forget my years, "the Generalissimo is one of us, Burtoni. Just a man. A sailor. A working merchant mariner, Burtoni. With calluses on his hands and shoulders broad from toting the rich man's freight. Unlike that one." He nodded his head toward Count Pilo, and Rosalino took it as a salutation. So he waved back at us, a big grand wave of the arm and with a lift in his step.

"Some of us, Burtoni, are not just common men," Corrao whispered. "No matter what they say. Some of us are 'Nobility.' Some of us come from a higher birth, with fine skin and soft hands, Burtoni, and so we can only trust them so far. We have to watch them and be careful that, when the moment comes," Corrao raised his arm and waved broadly back at the Count, "They don't just take over for themselves. I'm afraid many of these poor contadini would follow them right along, and just replace one king with a new one."

I was stunned by this talk and at first it made me laugh out loud. "Not our Rosalino, you don't mean. Corrao, Pilo's heart is brave. He has suffered with us, for us, for years. Why, it's because of him, his little lies, that the General is even here."

Corrao smiled and his face brightened and he said, "Of course, not Count Pilo of Grigenti. I'm not speaking of the Count," he said loudly and assuredly, "and his lies."

I gave him a puzzled look. But he just rose to his feet and saluted Rosalino.

"Giovanni, we have great news," Count Pilo shouted over as he drew closer. Then he looked down at me, "Burtoni, we have our orders to move!"

"The Bourbons are holding Monreale now," Pilo told us, once he strode up to us and then hunkered down on his haunches, near where I sat on the ground. "We have our orders. We are to maneuver up into the hills above them."

"San Martino," Corrao said, the Palermo street kid who knows the landscape now and understands the lay of it almost instinctively. He looked out over the surrounding hills.

Pilo grinned and nodded to him, "That's right, Captain Corrao. We are to take up the high ground near that monastery, with both of our squadrons on Castellacio. Then we just hold the King's troops down there, while the General and his brigade will march around them. He will enter the city from the south and the east, instead of where they're expecting him to come from the southwest, from Calatafimi."

"So our job is just to keep the enemy busy," I said, "to the southeast."

Corrao finished the thought, "While il Generale flanks them and takes Palermo from behind."

"The Bourbons will be trapped between us," I said. "It's brilliant, sir."

"But we are the key, comrades," Count Pilo said, his head nodding. "If we can hold them in Monreale, then Palermo is ours, and the Bourbon troops will be ours too."

Corrao laughed at that, and sat back down against a tree. "We're the bait in the General's trap," he said, with a smile on his face. .

That was when a short Sicilian man came running up the hillside toward us. "Dottore, Dottore," he was calling out as he ran.

I glanced around to see who this man might be calling out for, but there was no one beyond us on the hillside. Still the fellow kept running towards us, and now he was waving in our direction. "Dottore, Dottore," he called out.

A big grin spread out across Count Pilo's face. "Must be a lad from the Vucciria, eh, Giovanni?" And then Pilo started to laugh.

Giovanni Corrao squirmed a little where he was seated on the ground, but then he stood up again. To my surprise, the young fellow rushed straight up to Corrao, and grabbed him by the forearms. "Dottore, it's my brother, Dottore. He's cut his arm open with a bayonet. You must come now. He's bleeding all over, Dottore Calogero." I thought the young man had gone mad, or something.

But Pilo stifled his grin as much as he could, and then he said, "Dr. Calogero, do you need any help, sir?"

Again, I was glancing back over my shoulder to see whom I had missed, who else was present. But Pilo was staring wryly at our man, Giovanni Corrao.

"No, your lordship," Corrao said with a little ice in his voice. "I believe I can handle this."

"Dottore, we must hurry," the young fellow said.

"Yes," Corrao said, "Fine. Where is he?" And off they both went at a quick jog down into the encampment on the field below.

"Dr. Calogero?" I said, and looked over at Pilo.

That made the Count laugh in a happy way I'd not heard from him before. "Calogero?" I repeated.

"Oh, my Burtoni, there is a lot you don't know about our dear friend, Signor Corrao."

"But," I said, "Dr. Calogero?" And so I laughed too.

Pilo chuckled and shook his head a little, as he slid down from his haunches and sat just exactly where Corrao had been sitting moments before. He reached out, as he settled in, and touched the red shirt on my back. "It's good that you are wearing it, Burtoni. It will bring some dreams and some bravery into the hearts of these little contadini and picciotti, now, as we head into this war for real."

"It was Giovanni's idea," I said. "He brought it out to me." Pilo smiled thoughtfully and muttered Corrao's name a little wistfully.

"Who is this Dr. Calogero?" I said.

"Giovanni Corrao, my friend, has been many things." Pilo's smile was affectionate as he spoke. "You see, Burtoni, he was born in the Vucciria." He paused there, as if that would explain everything, and then he remembered I was not a Sicilian, had never before been to this island, much less to its capital city.

"The Vucciria is a neighborhood in Palermo, Burtoni. It's rough. It's always been rough. During the daylight hours, it is one of the greatest bazaars in the world; everywhere tables and tents, and you can buy or sell almost anything you want." Then he raised his eyebrows and repeated, "Anything, Burtoni. Almost anything you might want."

I nodded that I understood.

"But at night, the market disappears and another world comes to life in the shadows of the alleys and the narrow streets. Everything, Burtoni, is still for sale in the Vucciria. But the customers and the merchants have changed, and the tables are gone, and the dealing happens in the corners, away from the lights. And our friend Giovanni grew up there. In the Vucciria. His mother, well, she didn't know who his father was. Or which one, if you understand me. So he has only his mother's name."

From the way Count Pilo spoke I remembered what Corrao had said. I remembered his warnings. The Count is different than we are, Corrao had said. Our little Rosalino has an old and revered name, tied deeply to the Sicilian south. He is of 'higher birth' than we are, Giovanni Corrao and I. He is a Pilo di Grigento.

"But, Rosalino, this is what we are fighting for, isn't it? So that names don't mean anything?" I said, speaking not just to him.

Count Pilo smiles and nods his head yes, thoughtfully. "It is true."

"We are fighting so that every man can make his own name."

"Or perhaps," Pilo added, "in Giovanni's case, several names." Then he laughed again at something and went on. "This is why Signor Corrao is so useful to us, my friend. This is why we need him so. He is invisible, because he has been visible in so many ways. I don't even know, Burtoni, if Giovanni Corrao is his true name. Since I have known him, here in Sicily over the last 20 years or so, he has been Corrado, Corrani, Cerini, Ceriani, and probably a few more."

"And now," I asked, "he's a Doctor?"

"When I came back to Sicily, from Switzerland, from my first exile—it was ten years ago, I guess—the people in

Lugano, well, we won't use their names in case we need them again. But when I came back here, dressed as a peasant, I heard this name. Go to Palermo, get down in the Vucciria, and ask for Dottore Calogero. He will set you up. This is what our people in Lugano told me." I noticed Rosalino Pilo was staring out at the men in the field as he spoke. He seemed to relax and nestle into his memory. "So when I got to Palermo I asked around the market, and every time, before anyone would show me the way, they always glanced all around to see who might be with me, who might be trying to listen. Then they would tell me the name of a street. It always turned out to be just a side alley, with nothing there. So I thought, this Dottore must be a big man. Everyone is afraid to tell me who he is.

"Finally, after I came back to the market for the third day in a row and asked the same questions to the same fishmonger, once again he looked carefully all around before he spoke. He had a long blade in his hand, and he was slicing a thick steak from the side of a swordfish. He looked away from me and up at the fish's head with its long snout on display above us, and then he muttered quietly the name of a café."

I couldn't help but notice that Pilo never mentioned the name of this café or any of the names of the fishmonger or anybody else. Not even to me, who'd ridden this far with him and who was preparing to fight and maybe die at his side. Not even to me would he, after ten years, speak those names out loud.

That was when I realized that for Corrao, or Calogero, or whoever he was, and for Rosalino too, what he was telling me now had nothing to do with the General or this revolution. What he was telling me now had to do with this island of Sicily, with Palermo.

"Burtoni, I didn't say thanks, I didn't even nod in acknowledgement. The fishmonger, he just glanced at my eyes once, for just an instant. I didn't even think of repeating the name of the place he'd mentioned. I just gave him a little money and, loudly, he handed me a piece of swordfish, saying 'Grazie, Signore!' And then he began calling out his wares to the market again, as if nothing had passed between us but a piece of fish. I didn't look back as I strolled away slowly into the market.

"And so I wandered around in the Vucciria, through the alleys and side streets, and I shopped a little and bought some fruit. I gave the piece of swordfish away to an old woman on the street. And I looked and looked for this café. But it was nowhere to be found. And I knew better than to ask about it. The very mention of its name might make it disappear, or make me disappear.

"After dark, the Vucciria changes though. All the little shops and wide spread stalls roll up their wares and go away, and the streets fill up with people strolling the passeggiata. I wandered around, and I began to ask people where there was a café. Not any particular café, lest I be sent off with another wild misdirection. I just asked for a good café. Good local places for a coffee, maybe a sweet, a glass of wine. And so I was led off into some dark corners and a few blind alleys, and after about three hours of wandering around in and through the neighborhood, I came upon a narrow lane, not even wide enough for two people to pass one another with ease. A pale light shone out onto the stones of the alley, but it came from out of my view. I noticed people entering and leaving silently and quickly from there. They didn't seem to be wanting coffee, or a drink of wine. I walked down toward the light and found a sign bearing the name of the café. I know I had walked past two or three times during that day, and no café existed on that spot in the daylight. But now, in the shadows and the dark, it was there."

It was clear to me once again that the Count was carefully leaving all the names unmentioned, even to me, and even after ten years had passed.

"Inside there was a small crowd from the bazaar, and I ordered a coffee and drank it standing at the bar. It was odd, but no one spoke to me, though I tried to make small talk. So finally, I just asked plainly to see the Doctor.

"Suddenly everyone in the room stopped to look at me, and examine me up and down, but only for an instant. Then all at once the chatter began in earnest, about everything except the Doctor I'd asked for. How was the fishing? They said to one another. When would the olives be ready? How was the crop going to be? Who was trying to marry a signorina named Anita? It was as if I'd never spoken of any doctor, or even spoken at all.

"I finished my coffee, and thought to leave, but I knew from the way the people responded that I was in the right place. This was where the fishmonger had sent me. So I didn't order anything else, I just stood and took up space at the bar. Someone even offered to buy me a bitter; I turned it down and just stood and waited some more. After a while, a short dark man in the rugged clothes of a sailor approached the bar and muttered, 'Come with me, your lordship.'

"He took me through a back door to the office behind the little café, where another man sat on a chair in the corner, and two men with long knives stood beside him. He asked who I was, and what I wanted. I realized that if I didn't tell them something they wanted to hear, I would not walk out of that room alive. But I told him only that I came from Switzerland and I was looking for Dr. Calogero. I

131

didn't say my name. Perhaps by that time they already knew it.

"He listened to me, and then he listened to my silence for a while, and then he said to the long knives, 'Okay.'

"They took me from there out into a back alley, where we all knew they could easily have sliced me and left me to bleed to death, a place where no one would dare to answer my cries for help. Then we entered through another door and went up some stairs and finally we reached a room where an old, white-haired man sat reading from a newspaper. 'You are looking for Dottore Calogero,' he said flatly, but in a thick Sicilian that was hard for me, who grew up here on this island, to understand. His statement was not a question; it was recognition of a stated fact. I nodded yes anyway. He wanted only to know who sent me. I took a chance, and I said the names I knew, the aliases of two men in Lugano who'd sent me to Palermo. The old man nodded at each name, and then in Sicilian again, he ordered, 'Take him," to the two long knives.

"It went on like this for a while, Burtoni," Pilo said. "There were more doors and empty rooms, stairways and alleys. At one point we even crossed over some red tiled roofs and climbed from one building to another on a rickety ladder.   And then we picked up two more toughs, these were carrying straight razors and they liked to test their sharpness with their thumbs whenever they were still.   I answered more of their questions with the same few, bare facts. I never told them anymore than I already had, but it always was enough to move me on to the next set of stairs and through another doorway to more back alleys.

"Finally we entered a large room packed with people. A salon really, filled with furniture that was old and probably stolen.   There were children with their mothers, old workmen with only a few teeth left, a young and pretty girl ready to give birth. They were all waiting to see the Dottore, this Calogero, beyond a closed door at the far end of the busy, silent room.

"'Wait here,' one of the razors said, and then they went inside leaving me with the two long knives amidst the sick and poor in the salon. At first I figured it would likely be a long wait, but in just a moment or two, the door opened and out popped one of the razors. He looked me directly in the eye, and that look led me inside.

"'What did I find inside there, Burtoni?" Pilo began to laugh loudly. "First there was a little child, with his shirt off, and his mama tearfully touching him and standing at his side. The boy was sitting up on a table to be examined by the Dottore. And who do you think he was?" Count Pilo stopped and shook his head and muttered something I couldn't hear about a thief under his breath.

"Dottore Calogero?" I said, incredulous.

"Yes, Burtoni," Pilo said. "It was our lad Giovanni. Signor Corrao, Corrado, Coriano, all in one. Dottore Calogero."

"But," I asked, "is he really a doctor?"

"Well, let's put it this way, lad," Pilo raised his eyebrows and cocked his head. "I don't think our boy Giovanni has any papers from the University of Padova. Unless, of course, he bought them in the fish market, wrapped around a piece of tuna." Then Rosalino Pilo shrugged and said, "But those patients of his, they did believe in him, Burtoni. There must have been a few of them got better, after they saw . . ."

" . . . Dottore Calogero," I repeated, and then we both laughed.

"Get some rest, Burtoni," the Count told me after that. "Tonight after dark we move past Monreale to the Monastery, and then, lad, the real fight will begin. You'll need your rest soon."

Later, before we left the plain at dark that night, I told Rafaella this story that Count Pilo told me, about our Dottore. But she seemed more interested in the convoluted search it took to find Giovanni, than she was in his medical practice. "You're right," I said to her. "Why would it be so hard to find the doctor? Was he hiding his practice from the Police?"

"No," she told me, and then explained it to me from out of her own Sicilian roots. "This doctoring, that's just a skill he has, a talent. He's a healer. The police would leave him alone for that. But that's not all he is. He is a man of honor. The Count may have some royal blood in his veins, but I think our Corrao, he belongs to a different kind of blood. It's not his family name. But from his skills and his honor, and the way he is protected, our friend Corrao belongs to one of the 'families' who run this island. The Bourbons and their police, they think they rule here in Sicilia, but this land belongs to the families who really make all the decisions. And the way Signor Corrao is protected, trust me, my love, Giovanni Corrao is a much bigger man around here than he appears. Much bigger than Rosalino can even imagine."

"Corrao," I said.

"If that is even his name," Rafaella whispered.

21.

18 May
Monastero di San Martino, above Monreale

We arrived here two nights ago in the mountains that stand over the village of Monreale. The whole three hundred of us are arrayed now across the hillside looking down at the road below. As yet the troops of the Bourbons have not advanced out of Palermo toward us, so everything remains quiet. But if those troops don't find us soon, we will have to challenge them in some way, or our decoy will not work.

This morning Rosalino caught Rafaella and I returning from the village of Monreale at dawn. He had a big grin on his face as he watched us walk into the main encampment, hand in hand. I guess the change in me, in us, was obvious, at least to Rosalino. Our world is entirely different now; it has grown to a proportion I don't quite understand yet, and the Count can see this in us right away, even from a distance.

Rosalino pulled me aside, almost immediately, and I thought it was to brief me on the plans for the battle ahead. But instead he clapped me on the shoulder and then he held me tight and he told me how beautiful my Rafaella was with her hand in mine in the morning light. How could he know? I wondered. Then he surprised me.

"Burtoni, I don't think I'll ever see my Rosetta again." His eyes welled up with tears quickly. "When I see the two of you together, I know how much I have lost. I have lost her. Burtoni, this is very special, what you two have. You love her with all your heart, lad. With all your heart. Once this war begins, there is not any one of us who knows who he will ever see again."

"But Rosalino," I said, "You will walk with her through the free streets of Roma. I know you will."

"That's right, Burtoni," but his eyes were welling up again. "We'll all meet at Castel Sant'Angelo with the General, and we'll stroll to the Pantheon arm in arm, singing songs of the old Roman Republic reborn. All of us. Rosetta and I, Rafaella and you. Together, and free, in peace at last."

But then, without wiping his eyes in his pride, a tear began to slip down his cheek. "Take care of her, Burtoni. She is precious. Never let her down. Remember, nothing is worth losing her. Nothing." Then he shook his head no, and wiped the tear away, in order to silence himself.

He quickly walked away, and I saw Corrao watching the two of us, as we parted. We had come so far together, like brothers. I know we will never part. We will be free together. After this dark time, we will be free. After.

We must.

Last night, once the dark had fallen on the monastery, Rafaella came to me and, just as she did in Castellnotte, she took my hand and whispered, "I want you to see something." But this time there was an urgency that was new in her voice. "Before the battle begins, you must see this."

And so I followed her down a narrow foot path from the mountainside and at one point, when I could hardly see her in the darkness, I whispered out desperately, "Where are we going, Rafaella?"

She stopped and turned back. "I want you to see the most beautiful place in the world, my love. You must see the sunrise over the Cloisters, before all this war begins." At that, she turned and pressed on down the footpath through the pinewoods toward the village that slowly emerged below. There was not a single light anywhere, but under the waning moon, she led me down through the old stone streets.

We slipped silently around the piazza, with the tall grey shadow of the Cathedral above it. She knew her way, and led me over to a stone wall. We climbed on a wooden ladder over that wall, then crept over the tiles of the roof, until silently we landed on our feet, with a leap, inside an enclosed garden.

Rafaella took my hand then, and with her other hand she held a finger up to her lips to keep me silent. She led me over to a fountain that tinkled softly under the starry sky, reflecting the pale quarter moon in its water. There we sat on the damp, warm grass and slowly the garden emerged around me, as my eyes grew comfortable with the light.

We were stretched out in the corner of a perfect square, and within that square were four perfectly square little gardens. The old fountain where we lay was the only thing asymmetrical, though it was a perfect square too.

Slowly I saw that all around me, the garden was surrounded by a colonnade, made of pointed arches above paired columns. With time I began to see that, while every arch was perfect, and every pair of colonettes matched the form of all the others, they were all different too. Some were decorated with mosaics, muted by the moonlight. Others were carved with geometric patterns in the stone. And then I saw that some others had lost their mosaics, or part of the colored stones and glass, and had left behind the ghost-like shadows of their lost brilliance, swirling around and around up the pillars.

With time I began to see that these arches, some of them, had themes. One was decorated with horses at the capitols, another had lions, another little cupids, and some other bore saints with folded hands and mitered heads. And there were still others that simply showed an angular or a curving design. But all of these details were subtle, and disappeared into a grand unity that celebrated the whole of the garden as one perfection united.

Rafaella held me and we lay there together, keeping one another warm until the sun began to rise, and the shadows of the colonnade slowly grew sharper.

Then, before it was entirely light, Rafaella led me through a door and back inside, into the cathedral, dark and empty, with only the flickering lights of votive candles to show the way. She knelt down on the empty stone floor, and began to silently pray. The whole place, in the darkness, made me uneasy, but I stood next to her. After the way we'd been so close in the garden, I did not want us to be apart, though there were no prayers in my heart. Slowly, as it grew light outside, the light began to filter through the stained glass, and the church began to reveal itself to me, with its sweeping arches and grand heights. The ceiling began to sparkle with the gold, and mosaics came together out of the shadows, dark bearded faces with olive eyes like Corrao's, and women with black flowing hair like Rafaella's.

As I looked around above me at the miracle of the ceiling, I saw what Rafaella knelt before. It was a huge mosaic of the Christ figure, with his arms stretched out around the dome, the creator of all, embracing us all. There was a peaceful liquidity to his gaze, as if He was a well we could, all of us, everyone of us, fall into for sustenance and refuge. And the grand circle of his arms spread out and curled around, and centered the whole church, no, it centered the whole world in the reach of His embrace, and He held us all to His heart, in safety and love and in sparkling, golden light.

Then, into the warm vastness of that sacred, silent space, broke the sharp detail of a lone footstep. Just a scuffed foot on the old stones. But it shattered everything in its wake, and it echoed like a canon beneath the Pantocreator.

Captured, seized, stopped before the battles ever begin. Traitors, betrayers of the cause. All these thoughts rushed through my mind. We had, in our indulgence, in our love, we let it all get away from us, and now we were caught.

Rafaella heard it too, and she silently pulled me down on my knees, and I understood. We were pilgrims. Penitents prostrate before God. She did not need to say a word.

But I understood what she had forgotten, or ignored. I was wearing the red shirt. Whoever it was who had stepped into the vastness of that room, if they were Bourbon or Royalist, they would know the meaning of that shirt. It seemed so ironic now to be caught with it, this gift from the General himself, handed over to me by Corrao and urged on me by Count Pilo, all to inspire the hearts of the squadrons of Monreale. And now it was only a blazon on my chest to send me to an island prison, or maybe even to a firing squad.

He came forward out of the shadows, dressed entirely in black. His footsteps now tapped across the marble stones. Rafaella and I both kept our heads down in apparent piety. "Bless you, my children," he said, in a Sicilian tinged Latin.

"Good morning, Father," Rafaella said, looking up at the priest. So I followed her eyes. He was short, so short and swarthy that clearly he was a local. His hair was the same hard silver gray as Rafaella's father, and his face was deeply creased with worry. He said something in Sicilian, and I understood enough to know he was telling us when the Mass would begin. Rafaella answered him, saying we had to go. My silence told the priest what he wanted to know, if my looks had not already. I did not come from this island.

The father then looked me up and down, and then he spoke in flawless, unaccented Italian. "That is a bright color you wear, young man. Be careful. It may shine down here too brightly, if you know what I mean."

"I understand," I said, as Rafaella and I both got up on our feet.

He nodded yes, and then he raised one hand and made a cross over us, blessing us in gesture as well as word. After that, without saying more, the old priest turned and walked loudly back to the sacristy.

"Come," Rafaella said, making the sign of the cross. "He's telling us to get out of here," she said.

Silently, but very quickly, we left the cathedral by a side door and came out below the building. In the early light, she led me around under the walls of the chevet, ornate and beautifully patterned above us, and then we were soon at the upper edge of the village.

"Will he?" I asked.

"I don't know," Rafaella said. "I can't tell whose side he is on. But he did not want any trouble in his church."

We scurried up deeper into the pinewoods, and out of the morning light. Once we were hidden in the shadows of the trees, I stopped her so we could look down at the still sleeping village of Monreale. From this height, the cathedral and the cloister attached to it were truly a miracle, and I wanted to say this to Rafaella. I wanted to thank her for this beauty, and for the night we shared, but once we stopped and looked back, we both saw that not everyone in the village was sound asleep.

Down below that piazza, on the steep road that wound up into town from Palermo, there was a pair of soldiers, in blue Bourbon uniforms, smoking on guard duty. Rafaella and I both knew that if there were guards out, then a regiment or two could not be far behind. The movement of men had come up from Palermo. The Bourbons have taken our bait.

"We must get back up to the monastery," I said. "Pilo needs to know that the troops are coming. It has started." I turned to head back up into the pinewood, but Rafaella stopped me, for just an instant.

"No matter what happens now," she said and stared deeply into my eyes, "We are husband and wife now. Always." For a moment, I lost my way. I swear I did not know where I was. I moved toward her, to kiss her. But then she said, "Pilo needs us. We must hurry."

It was this that Rosalino saw in us, as we climbed hurriedly back to San Martino.   The grin on his face tells me he knows it all.

22.

21 May
San Martino

O What torture just a few hours can bring. How the world can change, in a moment. From the heights of my joy, to this. In just the flash of a gun barrel.

They came at us in thousands. And we, we are only a few hundred boys. Clearly they took the bait, and they were hungry, for the thousands came at us with a fury, believing they had the General in their grasp. And we held them. We did.

But O Rosalino. Can he make it?

No more.

Rosalino Pilo, Count of Grigento. O fine Rubiolo.
Farewell.

23.

26 May
Gibilrossa Pass

At dawn tomorrow we will enter Palermo, at the first light of a Sunday morning. The word has spread through the countryside, but the enemy seems still not to know where we will come from. We are in sight of the city below us, and all of us are united now with the General. Captain Corrao leads the squadrons, but now he is under the General's command.

Rafaella has turned and headed back for Messina, to send word to her father of our success, and so I am alone now. I am under Giovanni Corrao's command.

And Rosalino, he is gone.

His sudden death has taught me, taught us all, how quickly we can be gone, any one of us. No matter how great a soul we might be. No matter how brave we are. No matter how much we have done, nor how essential we are to the success of our great cause. No matter at all. I don't know if I will survive what comes tomorrow, in the great battle for Palermo. And so now, by firelight, in the near dark long before dawn, I must again put this down so all who wish to know can know the truth. For I was there, he was by my side. And even now, the wild accusations are flying all around us. Corrao. Some of the picciotti of Corleone, and a few others who will dare to talk openly, they say it was Giovanni Corrao. It was his bullet, they say. But I was there. So I must put it all down, even if it takes me the rest of this night.

*   *   *

The first charge of the Bourbons was ferocious. They came at us in thousands and thousands with guns blazing, rushing up the hill and everything was furious for a time. We had positioned ourselves in the stones and shallow hollows just below the monastery, and our lines held, because Pilo had placed us in this superior position. We are only 300, and they are ten times our number, but they fell under our fire, and it was clear that we could hold them as long as our ammunition lasted. And that would be enough time for the General to march round his way and to prepare to enter the capitol from behind them, with surprise at his side.

Pilo was wise, though, and told us to hold our fire, as soon as the Bourbon troops began to fall back. He led us fearlessly, roving from every placement to each position in the stones. Wherever the Bourbon charge came hardest, Pilo was there and he always stood firm.

After the first attack had been repulsed, we had only two wounded, and Corrao, or Dottore Calogero I suppose I should call him, was busy bandaging their wounds. A proud huzzah rose up from the picciotti. "Good work, comrades," Pilo shouted to us all, and shifted from placement to placement to watch for the Bourbon movements below us.

In a short while, the troops charged at us again, from a different side of the hill. They were fools, or led by fools. We were weaker there under the steep embankment, because they were more exposed across a shelf of shale. Pilo just rolled his rifles over to back up the men on the

144

embankment, and the poor Bourbon troops fell below us under our careful fire. We did not rain fire on them, we drizzled. But it was a deadly mist of fire. Not one of them even reached the rocks where we were perched in defense. They died at our feet without a purpose, and this time we took no casualties. Not one.

But we had still spent valuable ammunition, and all of us knew it. If they kept coming, the ugly time of bayonets would soon arrive. And we would have to hold the line with our lives.

After those two costly charges up the hills, all was quiet for a long while. But we knew it was not over. We had held the monastery, at almost no cost beyond the ammunition we'd spent. They could not know we were in short supply, after only those two assaults. So we held our fire and hoped they would keep taking the bait, and that fear of our superior position would limit their approach.

If it all fell into a slow siege, it would be the best. For the General and his thousand could round on them and take Palermo while we fended off the Bourbon attacks here at San Martino. But if they kept on bravely, we would soon be in danger of being overrun, and all would be lost. For us surely. Perhaps for the thousand. And then, for our dreams and our country.

But we had to put our brave faces on, for if the Bourbons grew weary of our defenses, and repaired to the edge of the Capitol, the surprise of the coming assault behind them would be lost. Pilo knew it was a delicate task put before him by the General. We had to appear vulnerable, but at the same time we had to hold our position.

Either a rousing victory that sent the Bourbon's fleeing, or a hasty retreat from our monastery, either might expose our Legions to a full attack of the Bourbon forces, just when the General was in his weakest position, with the Red Shirts sprawled across the mountains reaching for their advantage.

Pilo understood this, but he never spoke any of it. He was ready to die for it, with the rest of us. Perhaps he knew.

Sometime after that second assault, the disagreement broke out between Pilo and Corrao. Some of the talk now has made too much of this, I think, for it was not like they say. It was simpler than that.

Corrao announced to the Count that he was taking three men up the mountainside of Castellaccio. "They may be sending sharpshooters up there above us," he said.

"We need you here, at the line. The next attack won't be long in coming, Giovanni. I need you on the front line," Pilo answered.

"But, Rubiolo," Corrao said, using the old code-name he knew Pilo by in Genova on purpose. "If they get to a position above us, with even a few men, our advantage is lost. They'll pick us off slowly, until we flee."

Pilo paused and looked up at the two mountainsides above the monastery, Castellaccio and Giardinello. "I see," he muttered. In his head he knew, I think, that such an attack would be a good thing, for it would take a long while for the Bourbons to 'pick us off' from the heights. A long enough time for the General to arrive at the Quattro Canti in the heart of Palermo. He turned away then, and simply ordered Corrao, "Send five men up there to keep watch. But I need you here, Giovanni."

146

"But, Rubiolo," Corrao said, using that old name again, "it won't help us to know. Surely they are thinking of this, they can see Giardinello just as we can. We need to be prepared to stop then, if they try for it."

But Count Pilo just rounded on him, looking tired in his eyes, but he spoke slowly and distinctly, "Captain Corrao, I said send five good men to keep watch. And you will return to your squadron."

Giovanni Corrao glared at his friend, but failed to say "yes, Sir." He just wheeled on one boot heel and strode away, chin in the air.

This, you must know, is what the wagging tongues all saw. This is the moment they point to for their proof. Because Giovanni followed these orders from Count Pilo, but only up to a point. Not truly as Rosalino Pilo wished. Corrao took just four of his best men from his squadron, the best marksmen, the bravest hearts. He sent them out of the Abbey yard and up the steep side of Castellaccio above us. But the fifth man, the one who was not following his commander's orders, the one who led the other four marksmen up the mountainside, he called himself Comrade Calogero, the mysterious Dottore of the Vucciria.

It was later, after Corrao and his men were long gone, climbing up the side of Castellaccio, they say that Rosalino began writing to the General. He was asking il Generale to send help, and the letter he started with just his first word on the paper, was meant to warn the General of our dire situation, just 300 men before the stubborn onslaught of 3000. Send reinforcements to relieve us, to help us hold them off. Send the ammunition that even the Thousand were short of. Send them all soon, before the bayonets are unfurled. This is what they say he meant to write. This is what would be on that paper Rosalino never finished.

But I know differently. The one word he did write, it was not 'Generalissimo.' It was not 'Generale.' It was not even 'Piddu.' No.

The one word he wrote was: "Carissima."

Rosalino took me over to a scattering of broken stones at the edge of the old monastery. Two large rocks stand there, you can see them and the stains on them if you want. As we walked silently, he took pen and paper from an inner pocket of this coat. He sat himself down between the large stones, and smoothed the paper out on the flattest part of the stone he could find.

I was standing next to him, staring at the scene around me. I was standing right beside him, when he said his last words on this rugged earth. "Burtoni," he said, without ever looking up, with the pen in his hand and the inkbottle sitting on the stone. "I want you to take this, and get it to Rosetta, if something happens to . . ." His voice trailed off there, as if he knew what was coming somehow. And as if he had finally realized something about me, about my deceptive age, and about how I seemed always to emerge from great danger and survive.

But the stone he was trying to write on was too rough. Rosalino smoothed the paper this way and then smoothed it that way. If he'd only been writing a message to the General, that roughened stone would have been flat enough.

His scrawl, as long as it was readable, would have done for the necessary job.

But he was not writing a plea to il Generale. And so, Rosalino wanted that letter to look right. He stood up then and moved to the side, and then placed the paper on the flat of my shoulder blade. I bent forward a little to level the surface of the paper out for him, and he rested a hand on my back. If I had not bent over ever so slightly, perhaps I would have taken the bullet, and perhaps only in my shoulder or in an arm. Perhaps.

Then Rosalino wrote that one word on the paper, and said his last words to me. "If I don't make it out of here, Burtoni, take this to my Rosetta."

Corrao was right, you see. The Bourbon officers, whoever they are, they could see the futility of charging and charging and charging again up the hill into our fire and our bayonets. Some one of them could also see the advantage of Giardinello and Castellaccio, of pinching us off and trapping us beneath them, caught between the full army below us and an armed squad above us on the heights. But it was not just a few sharpshooters to heckle us. No. You see, during that quiet respite the Bourbons had moved a whole column of troops up from Monreale into the steep heights of Castellaccio, and quietly amassed their forces up there while we waited and watched for them to come at us again from below.

We first heard a scattering of shots from up in those steep hillsides, and then two of Corrao's men came running into our position around the Monastery walls, and they began to shout out a warning. "Above us! Look out! They have made the hillside! Up there!" Or something like that they shouted. I don't remember, because all of this happened in an instant. At once. It happened all at once, and in confusion. The hail of Bourbon fire followed hard on their cries. It poured down on us and chased the words of Corrao's men away from our ears.

Pilo looked up at the sound of their cries from his paper and his eyes passed mine as I glanced over my shoulder at him. But he was just turning back to see where all the shouting came from. There was nothing extraordinary in his eyes, no fear, no surprise, no fire, and no confusion. Nothing but a simple glance up, interrupting his words for a moment, as if someone had walked into a closed room. And then he was struck.

His face disappeared before my eyes. The bullet, or bullets, struck him straight on and turned his whole countenance into a sudden mass of red blood. He did not speak or even utter a cry. It all just fell onto him, like a bolt charging at him from some demonic curse.

His body became rigid for a moment, and he threw up one of his arms before his head uselessly. And then he went limp, and I caught him and held him up and eased his still struggling body down onto the ground. I think that I was screaming for help, but this I don't recall now for sure. I don't really know.

Later, after he was gone, I found the letter, the piece of paper with just that one word 'Carissima' written carefully on it, I found it stuffed in my pocket. Not folded. Just a crumpled ball of paper stuck in the pocket of my pants. Without even a speck of his blood on it.

I do not remember it falling to the ground. I don't remember picking it up, though I must have. I don't even remember thinking of it. I don't know how or when I came by it. But it was there in the morning. "Carissima." In my pocket. His last word.

The pen and the ink have disappeared.

Corrao was beside us almost immediately. Some of the picciotti say he was there too soon. It was almost as if he knew that the Count had been struck, they say. But together he and I picked Pilo up. The assault from below us rose then, and the Bourbon bullets rained down on us from the mountainside above. Someone, somewhere, yelled, "retreat," and that started it. The squadrons, with their leader fallen, were done and in disarray, and the men began to flee before the Bourbon charge and the battle, from the moment on, belonged to our enemies.

The Abbot of San Martino, a good man called Friar Ubaldo, came running bravely out onto that field of fire, when he saw that Pilo had fallen. There were two monks behind him carrying a litter. And so we hurriedly lay Rosalino on it, without a word between us, and then we fled, as fast as we could carry him, out of San Martino della Scalla.

On the backside of the hill lay a little village, just a few cottages grouped around a well was all. And as our squadrons vanished into the hills, disappearing, abandoning their arms, turning back into the local peasants as they ran, Corrao and I carried Rosalino inside a little hovel in that village called Niviera. The contadini there took us in and hid us far from the Bourbon troops ranging the hillsides behind us, hunting for the 'rebels.'

Rosalino was breathing steadily, and he lay still, resting easily. Corrao cleaned the wound and only then could we see how hurt he was. He could not speak or see, and he did not respond when we spoke to him. His face was gone, all the detail of it, the patrician nose, the piercing brown eyes, the curling lips that loved to smile, all gone. "Rosalino," Corrao spoke to him with great tenderness, as he held Pilo's hand. I placed my hand over the other one, but there was no response. "Rosalino," Corrao said. But the Count did not flinch or even move in answer. "Rosalino." And yet his great and brave heart kept beating, and he was alive still, lying quietly as sleep, breathing through the red wound that had replaced his face.

There are those today who say it was a bullet from Giovanni Corrao that did him in, that Giovanni wanted the Count gone, wanted his place in the General's eyes. But I am here to tell you they are liars. It was in that cowardly hail of Bourbon bullets raining in their thousands down all the way from Napoli to here in tiny San Martino that Rosalino Pilo fell.

You have never seen a dying man, lost to us already, comforted more gently that Rosalino was. Giovanni Corrao sat with him, I swear to you, and spoke to him quietly. He cleaned that wound that was once the Count's face so gently that Rosalino never stirred with discomfort. And Giovanni, he refused to leave Rosalino's side.

But as nightfall came, and the world began to grow quiet, Rosalino began to stir. His legs moved and kicked, as sweat of a fever began to wrack him, until suddenly he began to shiver violently. Corrao wrapped him in his jacket and in mine, but the poor people of Niviera had nothing to put around him and not even much to put in the fire to warm the dark room. Though truthfully, it was not cold, and I doubt we could have warmed the room enough to comfort poor Rosalino.

The Abbot Ubaldo, praying quietly for the Count in the damp corner of the cottage all that afternoon, said finally, "It is safe now. We must move him back up to the Abbey where we can keep his Excellency, Count di Grigento, comfortable."

"But he's too weak. He won't survive the move," I protested, tucking my tunic in again around Rosalino's bare squirming feet.

"Yes he will," Corrao interrupted my whining. "Rosalino Pilo is tough, and he is not easily departing from this war. He has started it, by God's own arse, he has. Now he wants to fight some more, Burtoni. Don't you see that."

So we wrapped him in everything we could and we carried him up on the litter to the warm stone rooms inside the monastery. I know that Ubaldo wanted the Count di Grigento to die in a sacred place, with the benefits of his church, and the Friar was doing his part to save the Count's soul. And I almost don't dare to say this here, because so many little tongues are wagging against Corrao, but Giovanni may have just hoped to ease his friend off quickly into the next world by carrying him up through the cool of the night.

"Dottore?" the Abbot said to Corrao, and then he led us out of the low door and into the early mountain cold.

Ubaldo brought us to a small cell just off the monastery chapel and there we laid Rosalino on a bed the brothers had carried in. They kept him under wool blankets and on crisp clean sheets, and they kept a great fire roaring in a fireplace in the corner. And right outside the closed door, in the chapel, the brothers chanted their prayers in a constant soft hymn for Rosalino's soul. They were treating him as if he was a dieing brother, a member of the order.

I remembered him, drinking heartily and laughing in the old Il Gufo sulla Luna, Rubiolo telling jokes to this Doctor Calogero and many others. I remembered the way he laughed at me when I saved us all by coating myself with Joan d'Arc's shit. And at one point, Corrao and I began to sing to him his own song about the heroes of old, the one he sang to cheer us on, when we were all sailing aboard the Speranza for Sicilia. And I was surprised when Ubaldo, getting a sense of the tune, knew the words and joined in with a smile. "Foscolo," he said, though I am still not sure what he meant.

It is hard to believe that Rosalino has come to this, lying senseless in a chapel surrounded by chanting monks, when just yesterday he was ordering the squadrons around and singing the praises of Liberta', and Italia, waiting for word from il Generalissimo.

Corrao said to me, "Burtoni, you go and get some sleep. I will stay with him. Tomorrow we will need our strength, and the next day, to ride with the General into Palermo. Just as Rosalino dreamed we would."

I protested again, but the Abbot stood up and took me by the arm and led me out into the chapel. "He's right, my son," Friar Ubaldo said. "There's no more you can do here. And after you've rested, you can return and let your friend get some rest too."

He treated me, as everyone does, as if I'm a boy. No one ever recognizes the length of my experience, the time that I have spent in life, the long run of history that I have seen. No, they see only the false youth in my face.

Everything I said to Friar Ubaldo made no difference. He led me out and closed the door, and we left Corrao alone with Rosalino in that small, warm room. So I went off to a huge dormitory, lined with rows of beds, and lay down to sleep. Yet before I could really close my eyes, Corrao was there beside the bed.

"Burtoni," he whispered to me, "our friend is gone."

I sat up in bed and moved to get up, but he held me gently in place with just one hand. Then the tears broke loose in my eyes.

"Burtoni, it is better this way. He did not need to suffer anymore." Corrao said, "Get your rest. There is no more for us to do for him now. But we will need you tomorrow in the streets of Palermo. This is what Rosalino Pilo dreamed, when he was with us. We must both be prepared."

I pushed that hand aside, and ran across the chapel and into that little room. The Abbot was there, kneeling at the bedside, praying. The oils and instruments of the Last Rites were beside him on a table, but he was already done, and putting them away. Two brothers were already cleaning the body for burial.

Friar Ubaldo looked up at me, nodded yes. Then he stood and took my hands in his. For a long moment, he said nothing, respecting the loss in my eyes. Then he quietly said, "We will take care of this, my son."

*   *   *

It haunts me, even if it was right, that only Giovanni was with him in that room, behind that closed door, when Rosalino Pilo died. If what I think happened, if it did happen in that room, then I should have been there to help. Giovanni could have trusted me, then and there. He should have trusted me to help. But he did not.

And I won't to write down here what has occurred, even though Giovanni Corrao and I, Jack Burton, will always deny it. I won't write it down here. There are already too many tongues wagging with lies and suspicions.

Now the dawn approaches, and I am rested and ready at first light to enter the city with Comrade Corrao at our lead. And Il Generale above us all.

Today we will make him the Emperor of Sicily. Today the dreams of Rosalino Pilo will come true, or Giovanni Corrao and I, Jack Burton called Il Rosso, will die trying to make it so.

For Rosalino. And for his dream.

III.

The loosed pages of Jack Burton's notebook end there. I leafed back through them, hoping to find more somehow. But that was the end of what the old nun had given us.

"It's not possible," I said again, looking up at Rob.

"No, it isn't possible," he said, smiling and sipping from his wine glass.

"But it is him, isn't it," I said, not really asking any questions. I had not one doubt this journal was written by Jack Burton.

Rob didn't answer me. He simply stood up from the table and led me slowly back toward the Domus Mariae, through the ancient stones of Ortigia.

Back in our room, I opened the tall wooden doors to let in the sea air, and on the silvery horizon past the rocking fishing boats docked below us, the lights of oil tankers glided across the horizon toward a distant shore. The world seemed a different place, gazing out of that old convent window on the ancient sea.

"Is this all there is to it?" I said to Rob, and he understood what I meant. On one level, I was just asking: Do we know if there is more to Jack Burton's journal? Is this all that he wrote? Did he stop there at the mountainside of Monreale, on the verge of taking Palermo with Garibaldi? But Rob also understood the broader feeling of my question too, the slow frustrations of always chasing after Burton, but never really drawing any closer. He felt those frustrations too, perhaps more pointedly than I did.

"You know what happened next, Mr. History Professor Man , don't you?"

I didn't need to answer him, but I looked from the shining Ionian Sea to the ancient stone fortifications abutting the island of Ortigia, and I said, "Garibaldi and his Red Shirts invaded Palermo, and then swept across the north of Sicily, stopping for a big fight at Milazzo, and gathering more volunteer forces as they went. Then they crossed the straits of Messina and marched slowly north until they took Naples, with hardly a fight."

"Where they met up with the King, Vittorio Emmanuel, and . . . "

" . . . and Italy was united. Sort of . . ." I interrupted him and looked over at Rob. "You know that's not what I'm talking about."

Rob laughed, and then he walked over and stretched out on his bed, kicking off his boots. "What you've read is all I've been able to get so far, brother." He put both hands behind his head, and rested against the bed frame.

"But I want to know what happened to those torn out pages? Not just at the end, but in the middle. Did somebody steal those pages? What was on them? Did Giovanni Corrao use them for a napkin? Was it Rosalino Pilo's grocery list? Or did it have the names of the squadron leaders listed? What's missing from there? And why?"

Rob just laughed at me again and I understood this is why he'd wired me to come. This is why I was here. "Take a look at the letter again," he said to me. "If you put those pages into that book, you'll see they fit perfectly, right at the end. He tore them out of the back of that journal, to write his letter to Rafaella."

158

"So you don't think there is anymore? This is it, this is all there is? "

Rob shrugged, "Remember, there are those missing pages from the middle. Where ever they might be."

"Whatever they are?"

Rob nodded his head. "Somebody who didn't want them in there, removed them."

"And what is that letter talking about, Roberto?   If you're right, and those pages come from the end of this notebook, then he wrote that letter after he finished this journal."

Rob nodded yes. "And what is it talking about?" He grinned again, "That's why you are here, big brother. You are the history man. And together we're going to see what we can find out. Now that you know, just like I said you would, that this journal was truly written by our man Jack Burton, now we can really begin."

"I never said I knew that this was by Burton."

"You did. You said it just now."

"I did not. It can't be. Do you know how to add?"

"I do. And it can't. But it is."

I didn't answer.

"And you, Will, you know it's true."

There was a long moment's pause, a silence filled with anticipation, and then we both broke into happy, raucous laughter. At long last, after 15 years of poking around, we'd located a real true trace of the man. He was no longer just a fragment of childish circus dreams. We'd found him again, Jack Burton of the Red Shirt. Lost to us since the days of our youth, we'd found him. In a way.

"Tomorrow morning, we find the old Nun and we start digging around to see what more she knows about our boy, Jack Burton," Rob said, "Burtoni, of the Red Shirt."

What neither of us spoke out loud then was the real goal of our search: to find Burton again, or to find out what happened to him. Perhaps he was at last dead and gone, freed from his impossible life, resting finally in his own haunted peace. Just a little slice of the great circus of history. But neither Rob nor I believed that. Could he really be gone? Completely gone? Somewhere, out there, old as the wind, he lived still. And Odd as it seems, that is what we believed. Burton lives, by God. Viva Burtoni!

In the morning, the spring sun shone into our room and woke me up. Rob was already up, studying that two-page letter in Italian. "Let's get some coffee," he said as I came to, hoping to hurry me up.

It was the pretty little nun who made cappuccini for us in the breakfast room. Her brown eyes sparkled behind a smile that would make either of us want to stay forever in Sicily. "What a shame," Rob said, and I just nodded my head and slurped the light foam from the lip of my cup.

"We need to see the Sister," Rob told the little sorrella.

"Sister Teresa?" she asked.

"Yes, we need to give her something back," Rob said.

"Oh, that old book she gave you," the little sorrella smiled her bewitching smile again.

"Oh, you know about it," I said, not asking a question, just stating a fact.

"Yes," she said, drawing the word out with hesitation. "But Sister Teresa is gone," the little sorrella said brightly. "She said you can leave that old journal with me. I will bring it safely back to her. But, you are not leaving now, are you?"

When she asked like that, who could dream of leaving Ortigia? But Rob stuck to his plan, "We need to talk to Sister Teresa, before we leave. You see, Sister, . . . "

"Oh, that will be a long while. Sister Teresa is gone on her retreat. She won't be back for weeks, and there is no talking to anyone but her confessor until then." The stern, serious frown on the little nun's face told us there could be no exceptions to the rule. "But you're not leaving?" she repeated.

Rob glanced over at me, and his eyes said, 'Okay, brother, you try.'

"Sister?" I said, "What is your name, Sister?"

The little nun smiled again sweetly at me. "Chiara," she said, looking over at Rob, too.

"Sister Claire!" I exclaimed with a grin, translating her name into flat Midwestern English.

"You know Santa Chiara."

After that weak exchange, I just pleaded with her in my most dulcet tones, "Sister Chiara, my brother and I really need to speak with Sister Teresa. I have to return to the university in another few days or so. Rob has to go back to work. We can't wait for her, Sister." She nodded her head at me, gazing at us with those big dark eyes of hers, and she began to pick up the empty cups and plates from our table.

"Can we send her a note, at least?" I said, now desperately. Could we really get this close, only to reach a dead end?

Sister Chiara shook her head no. "The Sister is on retreat. Only an emergency of the highest importance can disturb her prayers and reflections." But the little sorrella

161

was now wearing a tiny smirk on her face; she knew something she wasn't sharing

Rob interrupted us, "So what do we do, Sister Chiara?" Both of his hands were in the air, palms up and pleading. "Where do we go from here? Do we have to come back? What should we do, Sister?"

That just made the little sorrella laugh out loud. "O Signori, Sister Teresa told us that you would come looking for her, and not just to return the journal. So she left me some instructions for you."

The grin on her pretty face then made me feel foolish. I realized we had been played by the old nun, and by her lovely young accomplice. "Sister Teresa told me that, if you came asking after her, and only if you came asking after her, that I should tell you to go on the bus Wednesday to Castellnotte, and watch for Lombardo to get on, along the way."

"Lombardo," Rob repeated, the name we both recognized from the journal. Was he some kind of aged monster too?

"And what do we do when we find 'Lombardo'?" I asked.

Sister Chiara didn't answer me.

"Does this Lombardo have a last name?" I tried a different tack.

"Sister Teresa said you should tell him who you are looking for. He will know what to do." That was it. That was all Sister Chiara told us, other than where to buy tickets and catch the bus to Castellnotte. Or perhaps it was all she would tell us, at any rate. I suspect that her instructions from old Sister Teresa were very clear and firm. And so, there was no more to tell.

On Wednesday morning at 5 a.m., we were downing espressos with the incoming sailors at a fisherman's café near Piazza delle Poste. Then we climbed on the sky blue AST autobus for a three and a half hour ride to Castellnotte. Rob sat us down near the front of the bus, near to the driver, so that we could find our man.

"Signore, do you know a man named 'Lombardo' from Castellnotte" Rob asked the driver. He looked at the two of us, from one to the other.

"Yes, this bus stops in Castellnotte," he said, his face straight and all business, acting as if he could not make out our Italian. But he was not fooling us, or giving anything up.

"Will you tell us when 'Lombardo' gets on?" Rob asked.

The driver acted as if he hadn't heard.

About twenty minutes late, with the bus only half full, the AST pulled out of the piazza. We lumbered slowly across the already bustling Ponte Umberto and then wound our way through the dirty, 'modern' town of Siracusa. Every now and then, we would pull over at a stop, and a few more workers got on, handing tickets to the driver, and then wandering to the back of the bus. Almost no one got off. No one said much.

The industrial shipyards slowly gave way to the grey green countryside, and then rows of almond trees and citrus trees began to take over the landscape. Driving through the countryside, sometimes an old woman with an empty sack would be standing beside the pavement, at the entrance to a dusty, gray dirt lane. Without a gesture or a word, the bus would lurch down through the gears and pull to a halt, and the old woman would climb on board, without much more than a nod to the uniformed driver.

About an hour and a half later, the AST turned off the highway and climbed up a steep hill to reach the little stone village of Buccheri. We wound through a street so narrow the bus barely fit, but the few Bucherini on the morning streets just twisted to their sides with a practiced ease, letting the big blue bus slide past without a blink or a nod. In the little square, before an old church, we jerked to a stop, and then a dozen or so children piled up into the bus. Even with sleep still in their eyes, and the collars of their uniforms sticking out of light spring jackets like loose feathers, once they were seated they began to chatter in happy Italian like a flock of wild birds. Calling from one end of the bus to the other, squirming in their seats, moving around the bus to tease somebody or flirt with a boy. Then one of the old women from the side of the road would bark out a command, and all would be quiet for a moment that was followed by giggles and stifled laughs, before the squirming and wandering and flirting around the bus began again.

The driver turned the big autobus around inside that tiny square, backing up and pulling forward three times before he could get the AST turned about and then headed out of Buccheri. The whole time, as he deftly maneuvered the bus, the general pandemonium of school kids went on.

The driver calmly worked away, undisturbed. We knew he did it all twice a day and nearly every day of the week.

So then it was back down on the steep and narrow road until we reached the highway again. "I see now why it's going to take three hours," Rob muttered in English to me.

There were two more little towns we stopped at along the way. Vizinni was down a steep lane in a valley filled with almonds. Grammicche we watched for a couple of miles sitting up on a high hill above us, until we climbed up to it on another narrow horse cart lane, paved over for buses and cars, but built for mules and goats. In both of these towns we took on another half dozen or so children, and they began to call out to one another as they got on, some of them leaning out of the open windows on the bus, hailing to their friends that there was a seat at the back, all waiting for some new mischief.

Two young girls in their early teens, who got on back in Buccheri, kept looking at Rob and I, and then whispering to one another. At every stop, they moved around in the bus, always finding seats closer to us.

I nudged Rob with an elbow and pointed them out. It was his big smile and a "Buon giorno" that started them to giggling, and then it was clear they wanted to try out their schoolroom English on us.

"Where are you from?" the braver girl said, her eyes darting over at her friend the whole time. The English words sounded foreign and practiced in her mouth.

"Siracusa," Rob answered, emphasizing the Sicilian 'g' sound in his pronunciation.

That made them laugh at us. With our height and our weight, it was pretty clear we weren't from Sicily. "Are you from the United States?" she said, a little too clearly.

Everyone on the bus was now listening, and even all the schoolchildren were quiet, watching to see what might happen.

"Yes," Rob said in English.

"Where are you going?" the dark haired girl said. She was now braver and a little more sure of her English.

"Castellnotte," Rob said. "We are trying to find someone named 'Lombardo' from Castellnotte. Do you know him?"

The two girls glanced at one another, and a round of mysterious giggles trickled through the bus.

"Do you know this 'Lombardo'?" I repeated.

But Rob understood immediately that we had just run into that deep strain of Sicilian reticence, the same as what we got from the bus driver. No one here was going to hand anyone over to a couple of foreigners without first talking to our mysterious Lombardo, and letting him know someone was asking for him.

"Where are you from in the United States?" the fair-haired one said.

"Iowa," said Rob, though this wasn't true for either of us now. "Do you know where Iowa is?" he said.

And so we rode along on the AST across the Sicilian interior, talking with two young school girls about the American Midwest, both of us trusting that when the moment arrived, we would find our 'Lombardo.'

On the winding road up the hillside to Grammiche, suddenly, as if it was being drawn out of some deep inner pocket, Mount Etna rose like a smoking giant in the blue sky. "Look there," Rob said, pointing past the mountain. A thin line in the distance past the volcano divided the blue sky in two, and I realized it was the edge of the Tyrrhenian Sea at the horizon, just a slightly different shade of blue, edging in mist, where sea met sky past the great gray green mountain.

We wheeled into the main square of Grammiche, and another half dozen kids carrying their backpacks climbed on. And behind them, not wishing to squirm in the door with them came slowly a string of four women, each one carrying an empty shopping sack. Some of them stood in the aisle of the bus, as it was now getting full, and then called out to others, to friends already on the bus. "Marcella, hallo," said one short grey woman in a navy blue dress.

"Anna, how are you?" came the answer from somewhere back in the bus.

"The old man?" someone else said, "Is he better today?"

Marcella just waved her free hand down from her shoulder to her knee in disgust. She didn't say a word, but that made the whole bus laugh.

Then there was some chatter in speedy Sicilian that neither Rob nor I could understand. Rob stood up and I followed him, and we let Marcella and one of her friends sit down. She seemed embarrassed, glancing down at her feet a lot, with the coos and whistles coming from some of the little boys on the bus.

"Marcella," some boy yelled in very clear Italian, "Don't let Marco find out!" And that was followed by uproarious laughter, and Marcella leaned up out of the seat, her jaw set like a rock, and glared down the aisle at all the kids seated on the bus.

Rob nudged me in the rib and pointed out of the front windshield of the bus with a nod of his head. Three old men, all of them darkened by years in the sun, squat and round, not one of them five foot tall, walked slowly arm in arm across the little piazza away from us. When they reached the opposite end, they turned all at once and then locked arms again, and began the slow walk toward the bus, chatting to one another all the while. "They've been walking back and forth like that since we stopped," Rob said with a little grin.

"Since before we stopped," I added.

Rob nodded, still grinning.

"It's market day in Castellnotte," the shyer, fair-haired girl said in English, trying to start our conversation again.

"Oh, I see," Rob said to her.

The driver glanced back at his full and noisy bus, and then he revved up the engine, and it coughed out a little blue smoke. He was watching something out in the piazza then, and he shook his head grumbling. Then he stood up from his seat and hung out the open door of the AST. "'Bardo! Andiamo!" he yelled, and then clambered back up to his seat stiffly, without glancing back. The three little old men kept strolling toward the bus, not even looking up. With an angry "harrumph!" the driver tooted the bus's horn twice.

Eventually the three little old men made it over to the AST, and after a series of hugs and warm two-fisted handshakes, the tallest of the three climbed on board. The driver let out another too loud "harrumph" and shoved the bus's folding door closed with his lever. Then, with a blind nod at the old man, he began to turn the bus around so we could work our way out of the piazza.

The short brown man clambered up out of the stairwell onto the main aisle at the front of the bus, and then he leaned down to wave his farewell to his friends in the square. But they had already begun their arm in arm stroll back across the piazza. The old man shrugged his shoulders and turned again to where Rob and I were still standing in the aisle in front of him.

"Marcella, buon giorno," he said, and she nodded hello while she kept her eyes on the floor of the bus.

The old man seemed a bit confused, and he looked down the rows of filled seats to the back of the bus, at all the schoolchildren who were suddenly so quiet. He threw out an open palm, with his other hand he held a seat back for balance. "Miei raggazzi, come andati?"

That started a wave of chuckling and giggling through the autobus, and a few of the children piped up, "Buon giorno. Nonno!" But oddly, no one said the old man's name, the way they had called out to Marcella and Anna and to the others.

I looked at Rob, and he whispered, "This is our boy." And then Rob glanced down at our two friends, the girls with their schoolbook English, but they refused to look back at us, their faces stone still, gazing firmly out of the bus window to the piazza outside. Robbed nodded to me.

"Lombardo," he said flatly, without any hint of a question in his voice. The bus, if possible, grew even more quiet.

The little brown man, square and short with piercing brown eyes, didn't answer but a quizzical smirk wrinkled his mouth. The bus driver's head twisted just a touch as he listened in over the working engines of the bus. He, like everyone else on that bus, was waiting to see if Lombardo would answer, or if they would need to continue keeping him a secret. But Lombardo answered, "Yes." Then he paused and waited for Rob and I to identify ourselves.

"This is my brother," Rob said my name after he had named himself.

"Buon giorno," Lombardo said, the smirk gone. But his eyes were even more intense. After a moment, he said, "How do I know you?" meaning really how did we know him. Marcella glanced up, but not at us in the aisle. The driver leaned a bit farther over in his seat, and cut the engine noticeably.

"We come from Siracusa," Rob said, sticking out a hand toward him. But Lombardo didn't take it just yet.

"We were staying at the Domus Mariae," Rob went on. "Sister Teresa sent us here to look for you. She gave us your name, and said you would be here on this bus."

"Sister Teresa," he said, looking at us now as he leaned toward us, but he still didn't take Rob's outstretched hand. "What did she want?" he muttered.

I thought maybe this was the wrong way to go at it, so I butted in. "Actually, Signor Lombardo, it was the little Sister Chiara who sent us. She gave us your name."

Lombardo stepped back as if the bus had jolted over a rock, and his head leaned back as he looked past my brother at me in the aisle. Marcella almost turned around in her seat now to boldly look us over anew. And then a big wide grin spread across Lombardo's face.

The bus then did hit a bump in the road, but it was because we were wandering off the pavement. The driver turned straight back in his seat with another "harrumph" and fought to keep the autobus on the road. And that lead to uproarious laughter from all the schoolboys, followed by a few squeals and nervous giggles from the girls, and the boys, too, who would dare let on they were frightened.

"Sorrella Chiara," Lombardo said. "And what, my new friends, did she say?"

"She said we should take this bus to Castellnotte and ask for you along the way," Rob jumped in.

Lombardo seemed thoughtful for a long moment, and then he looked at me as if I was more trustworthy than my brother.

"How is she?" he asked.

His name was Lombardo Sciascia, he told us, pronounced like it was an old doo-wop song: 'Sha-Sha.' Once he had shaken our hands, the two schoolgirls got up and gave Lombardo their seats. Rob and I scrunched into the seat next to him and rode for the hour or so left to reach Castellnotte, talking all the way.

It was market day there, so the AST made a lot of stops at the roadside along the way, and more and more people climbed on board. The broad chatter in Sicilian that started then and grew louder with every mile was too quick and too strange for even Rob to follow. But we spoke to Lombardo in our best Italian.

The old man quizzed us carefully about Sister Chiara. How did she look? Did she seem happy? Was she healthy? He got a lot of information from us, and we got next to nothing from him. But that was all right. We knew our time would come. Neither of us said a word about Jack Burton.

When the bus pulled into a dusty station at Castellnotte, we climbed out with Signor Sciascia and, before we could offer to buy him lunch, he said, "Are you hungry?" Then he led us in the opposite direction, away from the market piazza where Marcella and her friends were happily headed. Instead we walked along amongst all the school children noisily headed up toward the old part of town. They were heading reluctantly to school. Where Lombardo was leading us, we weren't sure.

We seemed to wander aimlessly through a lot of narrow medieval streets and then Sciascia took us straight through a back door and into the kitchen of a little restaurant. There stood the Nonna, she was cooking, and there was clearly her son in an apron, and his two lovely teenage daughters getting ready to wait on the tables.

"These are my friends," he proudly announced and introduced us by name. "Gaetano here will bring us the best food in town," he said to me, with a wink.

That made the Nonna snort a laugh, since surely she was the one with the recipes. But Lombardo leaned over toward her and said, as if to smooth things over, "They come with words from our little Rosalina."

The Nonna crossed herself and the two girls looked up from their preparations and examined us anew. Rob just smiled. "Sorrella Chiara," he said, making the connection. But both Rob and I had noticed that name. It stood out like a tower deep in the oldest forest: Rosalina. None of these names could be mere coincidence. Not in this country. Not with these traditions.

One of the two girls led us out to a table then in the piazza in front of the restaurant. "Bianco o rosso?" she said, to which Lombardo rattled off a string of instructions in quick Sicilian. We sat in the warm sun, away from the shadow the cathedral cast across the piazza.

As I sipped the cool white wine that the girl brought us, and we ate slices of a hard white cheese and a deep red salami, I pointed up to the violent and beautiful porcelain copula over the door to the church. Rob nodded and said,

"Santa Lucia," and we were both remembering the description in Jack Burton's journal.

"Are the stairs still here?" I asked Lombardo, and he grinned and said, "Oh yes, yes," as if the thought of their disappearance was inconceivable. "You have been here before then?" he said.

"No, never," Rob said. "We have just read about it." He didn't say where.

At that Lombardo Sciascia seemed surprised. "We don't see many tourists here," he said. "Almost none. We are pretty far from Taormina and Cefalu." He took a drink of wine. "From everywhere," he said, a little wistfully perhaps. "It is quiet here," he sighed, "these days."

Then the food came, slices of swordfish rolled around a sausage stuffing in a light tomato sauce, married perfectly to the simple white wine. As we ate, Sciascia pointed up above the spires of the church to the rock standing over us all, and at the old castle that stood there. "Castellnotte," he said proudly, "where we get our name."

"Yes," Rob said, "Castellnotte. Is there still an orange grove there?" he asked.

Sciascia looked us over carefully, and we got a dose of his Sicilian reticence. Then, after a long, long moment, he said carefully, "It is still there. It has not changed much since that day."

I snuck a quick glance over at Rob, to see if he knew what day Sciascia was talking about. Our eyes met for just an instant, and that told me no. But maybe this was why we'd been sent here. Sciascia, with his native suspiciousness, caught that little glance between us, I'm sure. He grew simultaneously more reticent, and more talkative.

"How is it you know my daughter?" he said, and his eyes were on his plate.

"Your daughter," I said, and stopped eating.

"Rosalina," he said.

Rob was grinning then, as I slowly caught on. "Sister Chiara," I said.

So as we sipped the last of the wine in the warm sun of the piazza, beneath that bright and frightening image of Santa Lucia, my brother explained it all to Sciascia. The way we were trying to find Jack Burton, our old friend from childhood, and how that search had strangely led us here. His daughter Rosalina, the pretty little nun at Domus Mariae, had sent us to Castellnotte to see him, after we'd read the journal the old Sorrella had given us.

Sciascia was quiet through most of it. He interrupted Rob only once. "Sister Teresa?" he said, looking up from under his dark brows, when Rob mentioned the old nun. But that was the only time Rob paused to clear things up. "So that is how we know about the orange grove and the stairs to the sea," he said to finish.

"And does she seem happy?" Sciascia said at the end.

"Sister Teresa?" I said.

He shook his head sharply. He didn't need to know about her. "Rosalina," he said.

I looked over at Rob, and he shrugged one shoulder. "She seems fine," my brother said. "From what we can see. She seems well."

"She's a beautiful girl," I blurted out, forgetting for a moment that I was speaking to her father and that she was a nun.

But Lombardo loved that, a broad proud grin spread across his face and he rocked his chair back on two legs.

174

"Yes." He said. "Rosalina is a beautiful child." But then his face darkened again at some thought, and it seemed better to drop the subject.

"Can we see the Castle?" Rob charged ahead. "Is it open still?"

Lombardo Sciascia stood and rubbed his hand through his short steely hair, and then he stretched a little in the sun. He seemed a bit hesitant to take us there and he said, "It is closed now." But with a jerk of his head, he got us up and led us back out of the piazza. "La Rocca will be open tomorrow. Part of it. Not the gardens, of course, but part of the castello, tomorrow. You see, it is being restored by the government. La Rocca is now a piece of our history, they say. Even if for a long, long time, we were all silent about what happened up there."

He spoke as we strolled through a narrow stone street. "What happened there?" Rob said finally.

This brought Lombardo up short, he turned and looked us over again. "I thought that was why you were here."

"We're here because your daughter sent us here," I said.

He snorted a laugh like the Nonna's in the restaurant.

"We're looking for Jack Burton," my brother said.

Sciascia nodded his head yes and turned back and led us out to a walled ledge. As he sauntered along, he said over his shoulder, "This journal, do you have it with you?"

There was a short stone wall about knee high to a Sicilian that curved around the edge of the square, and we looked from there out at the blue sea to the north. Mount Etna and the Castellnotte stood on the heights behind us.

"I have it right here," Rob pulled it out of his shoulder bag, the leather bound notebook tied up with leather strings. He handed it over to Sciascia who took it and turned it around in his hands. But he didn't open it. He couldn't read it, because it was in English anyway, but clearly he knew what it was. And what it meant too, though we were not yet sure ourselves of that.

"Our La Scala starts from here," he said, pointing with the hand that didn't hold Jack Burton's journal. "This is what Signor Burtoni saw the first time he came here, with Rosalino Pilo and Giovanni Corrado."

"Corrado?" Rob said. "But Burton calls him 'Corrao' in there," and he put a hand on the notebook, while glancing over at me for verification.

Sciascia just grinned, and then said, "It's good that you recognize him under that name. They say around here that the old Dottore was a man of many names, I'm afraid. Here, we call him Corrado. That is his real Sicilian name, you know, though all the history books get it wrong."

I stepped through an opening in the little wall and down a few of the old, uneven steps. When I turned and looked back up, I saw the first few of them. "Rob, you've got to come see this," I called out. Then I scurried down a half dozen more stairs.

They were just as Burton had described them. Every step was pure white and every tile was painted with bold red and blue and yellow figures. Simple, rustic designs, fishes and flowers and boats and human faces. And just as Jack Burton had written, they were hidden from above. You saw nothing but a twisting row of graveled stairs with a few hints of white ceramic edging when you looked down to the seashore. It was as if these artists were afraid to compete with the blue of the beautiful sea. But when you looked back up toward the village, toward their home, it was a true, dancing riot of color.

I admit, they were so beautiful, Rob and I left Sciascia with Burton's journal at the top and we ran all the way down the stairs to the rocky shoreline, so we could see them all, the reach of them all together, and then we slowly worked our way back up every step, admiring each and every one.

From the shoreline, the majolica stairs curled upward slowly and led your eyes directly to the façade of the church, where the ceramic of Santa Lucia was just an accompanying pinnacle of color, its violent martyred subject only a bright abstract design, like the painted stairs. Overshadowing it all, on the rock face above it, stood the vast honeyed walls of the Castle. La Rocca di Castellnotte.

Rob and I stood there on the dock at the bottom looking up wordlessly, both of us remembering Jack Burton and his Rafaella standing just there, where we were, with all their newborn love, pledging their eternal faith in one another.

But where did it lead them from here?

At the top of La Scala we found Sciascia sitting on a bench waiting for us, in the shade of an old olive tree. He was paging through the journal, though he couldn't read its English, he was gazing down at the handwriting, touching the old letters of Jack Burton's hand. Something in him had changed while we were gone. He seemed softer, gentler, and older too.

Since we couldn't see anything of the Castello until morning, we began to ask about a hotel. He smiled quizzically at us, and led us through the piazza under Santa Lucia's peaceful, upward cast eyes and then out to the edge of the village. "You have a place to stay," he said, in answer to all our questions. "You have a place to stay."

His house was a little three-room building made of stone on the edge of the village, with a clear view of La Rocca above, though his view of the ocean was blocked by a row of painted stone houses on a rise in the ground behind him.

He fed us with simple bread and salami and lots of wine. After the big lunch, it seemed plenty. Then he said, "I will stay in Rosalina's room, and you two will have mine. The bed is bigger. And in the morning, we'll go up to La Rocca, the castello. The three of us will go up, together."

In his room, on the whitewashed wall across from his bed, two pictures hung. One of them we recognized immediately as a photo of the young Rosalina. There was Sister Chiara, smiling and holding a doll, a beautiful young girl about to blossom into womanhood. She must have been twelve or thirteen years old, I'd guess. Nothing about that picture told you this child would grow up to become a nun. I don't know, really, if any photo could show a sign of that future. But if I hadn't known her as Sister Chiara, I would not expect this lovely child to be joining a convent soon.

"Oh, you're just showing your American background, Will," Rob said when I mentioned it to him. "You can't tell that kind of thing from a photograph."

Next to Rosalina's photo hung another photograph, black and white, of a young woman in a simply cut dress with a bouquet of flowers in her hand. She stared deliberately into the camera, and on her lips there was a quizzical smile, not forced but more than a bit confused. There was a shyness evident in her, not clever but genuine, and it drew the viewer in. This woman, standing alone in the village, was the very image of Rosalina Sciascia. The woman in the picture had to be the little Sorrella's mother.

Lombardo strode in, with a quick rap of his knuckles on the doorframe to announce his presence. He found us examining the pair of photos, not matching but alike, on his wall.

"Sister Chiara?" I said, with a nod to the color photo.

"Yes, that's my Rosalina," Lombardo said, "A happy child, she was." He was smiling. Then he stepped over and placed two fingers on the photo, "And this is her mother, my sweet Rosetta. Gone these many years." He made the sign of the cross and muttered silently some prayer.

"Rosalina looks just like her," Rob said boldly.

"She does at that," said Lombardo. "When she was little, after Rosetta was gone, sometimes little Rosalina would frighten me, how much she seemed like her mother. The way she walked. The way she laughed. It would surprise me."

I wanted to ask him what happened to Rosetta Sciascia, but it seemed at that moment prying and we were really strangers still, though it was seeming harder and harder to believe this.

But in the next moment Lombardo changed the subject entirely. He pulled a crisp manila envelope out from under his arm and handed it to me. Rob leaned toward me trying to see what it was. "I think this is what Sister Teresa has sent you here for, though I'm not sure why," Lombardo said.

"What is it?" I said.

Rob pointed at the front of the crisp envelope, where someone had written in a black marker 'G. Corrado.' But he didn't say anything.

"You read Italian?" Lombardo said, and we both nodded yes. "Good," he said. "Inside there is the letter your 'Corrao' wrote to Rafaella Crisiana explaining to her what happened here. This is what I think Sister Teresa wanted you to find here. This is why she sent you to me."

"How do you come by it?" I asked, confused as usual. Rob nudged me in the ribs, trying to say: Be Careful. Doors were opening all around us. Don't spoil it now by shaming them silent with too many questions.

Lombardo just smiled at me. "My Mother, who was named Rosalina too, like my daughter, passed it down to me, as the oldest child in the family. You see, Rafaella Crisiana was my grandmother."

Rob and I stood there, I suppose like gaping idiots, letting all this information settle in. It was hard to put all of it in place right then. It was too much, too fast, suddenly. Sciascia waited only a moment before he added, "You fellows read through this letter, and in the morning we'll go up to the castello. This is what, I guess, Sister Teresa wants us to do. She wants me to take you to La Rocca. I don't know why."

Then he turned slowly away and shut the door behind him as he wished us both a "Buona notte" and added "A domani" too.

A white string bound the manila packet shut. I fumbled around with it to get it open until Rob took it from me impatiently. He pulled it open quickly with a practiced hand, and inside we found a sheaf of loose yellowed pages, covered with a beautiful blue ink, in a hand that carried a great deal of flourish. Though the pages had yellowed, the ink had not faded at all. It was clear this document had been handled carefully, and not often, then stored safely away for at least a hundred years.

"Bingo!" Rob said, as he pulled out the first few pages gently. "This may be what we are looking for."

So we stretched out, side-by-side, both of us sitting with our backs propped at the head of the bed, and we passed the pages gingerly to one another, careful of their fragility and incomprehensible value. If any of the Italian was hard to make out, between the two of us we were able to read it without a dictionary. Most of it was written in a very formal and learned Italian without even a trace of Sicilian, or any other dialect for that matter. Perfect Tuscan, it was. And so it was easier for us to understand than, say, Jack Burton's letter to Rafaella. Or maybe it was just that our Italian was getting better with time. At any rate, we read straight through it to the end, with only a few stops when either Rob or I would say, "Does this mean what I think it does?"

Here follows then a text of what Giovanni Corrao wrote, in my rough translation from his Italian. I have tried to catch the flavor of his formal but passionate voice, though in that attempt I think I have failed. You will notice, I'm sure, his propensity to capitalize words for emphasis. I have left those capitals in place. There is no date on the document. It begins:

Signorina Crisiana,

I hope that this missive finds you well, or as well as can be expected under these Dire and Darkest circumstances, dearest Rafaella. I have undertaken to write to you at the request of our friend (at least I hope you still think of both him and of me as your friends, for we truly remain so) Sig. Giovanni Burtoni, also known as Jack Burton to some. He felt, as he reported to me, that you might find it more acceptable to hear this explanation from me, than from his pen. I truly don't know why he believes this, but since I too was sent at the head of the operation to Castellnotte, I can certainly report and verify as to the events that occurred there a year ago last August, why they happened and what befell therefore. Some of these things you know, from report or from experience I suppose, but I would like you to have the full and complete facts about these serious events, which have had such dour impact, as they occurred. Without any varnish, I might add.

In order for you to completely understand the actions taken at Castellnotte, as you were at that time resident in Messina, I believe, I must go back to the beginnings a bit, I'm afraid, and describe for you, in the very least, the conditions in which Sig. Burtoni and I found the city upon our arrival.

After our victorious action at Milazzo, we had marched toward Messina with the Thousand, as they are already known. Once again the nearly miraculous tide of battle had turned in our favor, as it had in Palermo, and as it had not so many times before in the past. The Fate of History, my Dearest Rafaella, seemed at last to be running with us, and not biting at our heels. And you were among those of us who had struggled to urge our History forward, to make that History break into a full run. I shall never forget your courage at San Martino when we lost our mutual friend, our dear Comrade in arms, our commander, that great spirit of the Revolution itself, Rosalino. It was you, Rafaella, who roused us then from the fear and stupor of our loss to urge us Onward, Burtoni and me, reminding us of what the Great Pilo himself would want. He would expect us to Press Forward without him, in his very memory, as it were. It was you who brought us back from our despair. And soon we rode with the General into Palermo.

But as we marched on to Messina, which the Bourbons had already abandoned, fleeing on their ships across the straits, we began to receive word of a rising in the mountains. The General had been declared, by acclamation of the Thousand, and by the freed people of Messina, to be the Dictator of Sicily. He was now the full and true ruler of the entire island.

It was his officer, our comrade in the liberation of Sicily, Nino Bixio who at word of these revolts in the interior took young Burtoni and me aside. "We must maintain order now," he told us, frankly. We dared not let Anarchy reign across our new Sicilia, across any part of it even, in the absence of the hated Bourbons For if we did let wild Anarchy rear its head, with its comrade Revenge, all might be lost.

"Take the dozen men at your side, the Heroes of Milazzo, and go out and restore the general order," Bixio commanded us. So it was we were sent to your dear Castellnotte, O Rafaella, with orders to bring these campagnolo revolts under Control and to a Definitive End. But this was not all, I'm afraid. Commander Bixio made our orders very clear, Rafaella. He was explicit in his commands. "You must execute the ringleaders, gentlemen," he said. "They must quickly be made an example, or once again, men, all we have struggled for will be lost."

This "All" that he spoke of, Rafaella, it is our very Country. This is what Commander Bixio meant.

Burtoni and I understood why we were being sent. Because of what we did, with you and with our late, lost Pilo, we were being entrusted with this Crucial if odious task. And I have no doubt, even now, Rafaella, where these hard orders came from: They came from il Generale himself. [At this point, Corrao had underlined the General's title with a forceful line, so I leave it in Italian.]

And so it was we set out on horseback with a dozen of the hardest, truest men at hand. In haste, we traveled with the urgency of the General in our minds, and with the dream of our country in our hearts.

It took us only a day, long and arduous as it was, to cover the hard ground beneath Etna and we reached the outskirts of Castellnotte at barest daylight. At first all seemed orderly. Though the people were lying about the piazza, sleeping off the excess of their celebrations, at dawn everything seemed in Order. The cathedral and the beautiful stairway to the sea, which you know so well from your childhood days, they were clean and shining in the morning light, as if they'd been washed by a purifying rain. All was calm and restful. Yet something was amiss, and it took us only a little time to find its roots.

As we rode into the piazza, some of the sleeping revelers began to stir. "Who is in charge here?" I asked repeatedly, to several of these waking and groggy men. At first they were able to answer with no names, they just looked at one another in a stupor that might have been sleep and might have been drink, and yet might again have been deceit. Certainly, with what I know now, it was all three.

It was Burtoni first who saw the problem. Perhaps it was because he had come to know this village with you at his side. Or at least this is what he told me, on our ride across the Nebrodi. On the step mountainside above us stood the Castle itself, you know it very well. Like a second home you know it, Burtoni claims. From that tall stone edifice, melded out of the rocks of the mountainside, there drifted upward a thin spire of black smoke. "Do you see it?" Burtoni said. And I did indeed. The Castle had been burned down to the stones, enough days before so that only the trace of smoke still wafted upward into the sky. It was, I suppose you would say, still smoldering. So you see, the reports were true, and our Hopes that they had been exaggerated died with that sight, O Rafaella.

We rounded up the men in the piazza and marched them inside the church. They were complacent, like weary sheep. It is dark and ancient inside that little cathedral, as I'm sure you know from many a winter Sunday morning. Light slanted in through narrow stained glass only faintly, though it was a bright summer's morning outside. But inside there were only shafts of colored light in a dusty air filled with old hints of candle smoke and incense. We were met with silence at first, but then I began to question them in Our Sicilian language, translating as I went for Burtoni as I spoke. Everyone else in our force knew this language as their mother tongue. And the sound of our own tongue seemed to loosen theirs.

"Comrade Tre," one of the men said finally. "He's in charge."

"And where is he?" I said, still in Sicilian.

They answered me with a lot of shrugs and glances at one another, until one of them muttered something about the stables. I only needed to nod to Burtoni, and he was gone, for you know, he was familiar with the village at least a little.

After that, it was silent in the cathedral. The villagers refused to speak at all, and I switched back into Italian, which I knew they understood. It is, after all, the language of our country. "So who is Comrade Uno?" I said, but at that they wouldn't even raise their heads.

Burtoni was gone for a long while, perhaps half an hour, and in a little village of that size, that is a long time. I began to ponder sending some of our dozen out to check on him, when finally he strode back into the church.

He was not alone, Signorina Crisiana. He brought back with him someone who I take it you would know well. And Burtoni was visible shaken, his eyes blank and dark with anger, but his shoulders drooped with a strange sadness. Beside him there was a young fair-haired lad of twenty or so. His hands were bound behind his back, and Burtoni shoved him in front of me and snarled at the boy, "On your knees, Gaetano," he said. The boy looked up at me fearfully, and Burtoni said flatly, "This is your 'Comrade Tre.'" But then Burtoni seemed to collapse into a pew seat and he covered his face with a hand.

For a moment, I didn't speak. I waited for these villagers to react or for someone to come forward. The lad just trembled like a puppy, kneeling before me. It was hard to imagine him as the leader of all these men, and not for a moment did I believe that he was.

Burtoni rose to his feet again, glared at all the village men around him in the church, took a deep breath, and then spoke out calm orders to our men, not to let anyone leave the building at any cost. Then he simply looked over at me and said, "You'd better come up with me and see what they have done."

It was as we strode up La Rocca toward the smoldering castle that he explained to me about you, Signorina, and the Duke and Duchess of Castellnotte, how they had raised you after your grandfather died and when your father went off to the university in Messina. You grew up in this tall castle, and the Lord and Lady Burmonte were like a doting aunt and uncle to you.

"And who is this young Gaetano?" I asked Burtoni.

This is when Burtoni told me, O Rafaella dear, of your plans to marry, of your vows on the Scala to one another, and of the way the Duke and Duchess had jumped with a truly parental joy and excitement to plan your celebration. Neither of you ever spoke of this to me, not even as we marched behind the great Pilo, and then with the Generale, across this island, taking first Palermo, and then the fortress of Milazzo and then to Messina. It was obvious, of course, that the two of you were deeply in love, as we might say, with one another. But never from either of you came a word of these plans, of this Marriage.

I know, Signorina, it was wartime, and certain hopes and dreams are better left unstated in times such as ours, when we are all preparing for battle, preparing everyday for the best of all possible worlds or for the worst that anyone can imagine, at the same time. But knowing of this vow or yours, I suppose, is what motivates me to report these sordid events to you as carefully and completely and honestly as I can. I cannot pretend to understand what has fallen between you and good old Burtoni now, but I can try to make clear the circumstances this Good Man struggled under in those days at Castellnotte. And so, I'm afraid, O Dear Rafaella, I will present you with the ugly details. All of them.

"Gaetano was one of Lord Burmonte's servants, a favorite," Burtoni told me. "Gaetano fed us and showed us our rooms the night we stayed here in the castle. Rafaella has known him since he was an infant." This is what good Burtoni told me as we marched together up the mountainside to the castle.

Burtoni stopped as we approached the stone walls at the crest of La Rocca, and spoke without looking at me. He seemed to be steeling himself for what awaited us inside those walls. "Corrao," he said to me, "do you remember the horses we rode, the fresh good horses Rafaella and I rode from here, to catch up with you and Rosalino on the way to

Pieni dei Greci. It was Gaetano. That lad was the one who gave us those horses, all rested and ready, and he said to me then that though he wanted to come, he couldn't come with us to meet the General. But he could give us those fine, fast horses to ride. They were the pick of the Duke's stables. He sent us off with them, because he couldn't join us."

I don't know if this is true, Signorina, but I know that Burtoni believed the boy Gaetano was one of us. And you don't need to be told. You know what the truth is.

Without another word, Burtoni led me up into the Castle grounds. The brassy stone walls still stood tall, and above us I could see that some of the floor work and the furniture was still inside, but the roofing was all gone in the blaze, and the belly of the Castle was charred and exposed to the now harsh morning light.

He led me around through some broken windows and charred doorways into a little square, once a secret interior garden cloister within the Castle. I don't need to describe for you this quiet place, Signorina Crisiana, for you know it well. Our Burtoni told me later that this was The Garden of miniature orange trees hidden away inside the wall, and you had shown him this place yourself in those passed and Better days of your love. This was where you hoped to speak your vows to one another publicly, Burtoni told me, in a lovely, peaceful garden where you had whiled away the summer hours as a child. Let me tell you now what we found there, so perhaps you can understand our dire actions later. Perhaps it will help you to understand.

The walls of the portico around the garden had remained mostly untouched, which told me that the fire in the castle, or most of it, had burned above us. The old citrus trees, which Burtoni described so clearly for me, were all gone, every one of them, though I could see the stumps still resting low in the fitted octagonal stones around them. I could see that the stone floor of the garden had once been designed around them. But now, you see, they had all been cut down and then heaped in the center of the cloister, where the central tree had once stood. Now, there only stood a heap of the charred remains of burnt trees where the bonfire had blazed.

I hesitate to tell you the next part of my report, O Rafaella, for it is distressing yet to me, and I did not know these people event to see them, much less know them as you did, as nigh unto Family. But even for me, it was a horrible sight, Dear Signorina. I am sorry to report it at all, especially to you, but again it may help you to understand our subsequent actions there in Castellnotte. It was not just orders we were following, I am afraid. I must confess to you. We were not just following our orders.

They were burned beyond any recognition, truly just the charred remains of two bodies down there in the still smoking charcoal of the lost orange trees. From the way their remains were still arched, it was clear that they had been bound hands to feet behind their backs. I don't know this for sure, and when we interrogated the townspeople later, no one would say. No one, I tell you. No one. I pause here again before I write it down now. But it seems to my eyes there was no reason to bind these victims in this way unless, I am sorry to say this here, O Rafaella, unless they were still alive when the branches of the orange trees were set ablaze.

"Who are they?" I asked Burtoni.

"I don't know," he answered me, "but I'm afraid I have an idea."

Burtoni stood there for a moment, not a praying man, but we were both searching for some prayer to say, though nothing came to us. "I can't believe Gaetano did this," he whispered after a while.

We walked back down to the church in silence. There was nothing to speak about, really, and we both of us Burtoni and I, we knew what our orders were. We did not have to plan. But this did not make what we were ordered to do any easier to follow, and yet our orders were clear from the start.

We took each of these men then back into the small sacristy, removed from the rest of the guarded villagers, one at a time, and Burtoni and I interrogated them. It was clear before long who those two bodies were, just as Burtoni had feared. They were the Lord and Lady Brumonte. And we heard stories that seemed to mesh about the servants ransacking the Castle. But no one knew who had bound the Duke and Duchess hand to foot and burned them alive. All their stories ended with confusion and doubts and ignorance, and just plain silence.

That is everyone except Gaetano. He alone laid claim to their horrible deaths. "You didn't do it alone," I said to him. "Yes," he answered, "I did." And then he would say no more.

It left us in a delicate position. We now had twenty some sheepish men under arrest, all of them guilty in one way or another, but only Gaetano would lay claim to the murder: 'Comrade Tre' as he called himself. We were here for an execution, though none of these men knew that, or would believe it if they were told. If we followed orders, executing the lot of them, all twenty, we knew we would be gutting the future of this little village. This was the heart of their manhood, half the soul of the town's next generation, indelibly altered forever. These were the fathers and the brothers who would raise the next generation. To take them all to the firing squad—though perhaps they merited it—would leave the women of Castellnotte with the young and the aged to care for, the fields and the herds to work. They would do it, but it would be a cruel and useless act remembered bitterly for generations. And you know, Signorina Rafaella, because you come from this island, are of it as I am, you know how long the Sicilian memory lives. No, Signorina, it was the ringleaders we needed, the one or two who were the true instigators. To execute them, the two or three who led the way, would leave Castellnotte in Order, Strong and Ready to Rebuild. And the message would be sent to everyone, all through the island. This kind of dangerous Anarchy, this Retribution of the common people on the aristocracy would not be tolerated. We need all of us, lords and peasants, ladies and maids, all of us to make new country. Our New Country, O Signorina.

But only Gaetano would lay claim to what had been done there. Everyone else was silent. All twenty or so men were just mute and dumb. Burtoni pulled me aside and we spoke quietly in the sacristy, away from all the other ears, both the villagers' and ours.

"What do we do now?" Burtoni said. I didn't answer, because I wanted to see what he would decide. After a long moment of silence, Burtoni just went on, "Gaetano didn't do this. He's taking the blame to hide someone else."

"Come with me," I said to Burtoni. So I took this young Gaetano by the arm, and with Burtoni following behind us, we marched back into the sacristy behind the altar. It was a little dark room filled with dark wood cabinets that were filled with bright vestments. I sat this Gaetano boy down on the floor and then I spoke into his face, leaning down to glare at him. "All right, Comrade Tre," I said, softly and putting a great little twist on his assumed title. "Do you know who I am?"

And so I talked to him then, talked to him in a way I knew, Sicilian village boy that he was, a way he would understand. You know it too, Signorina, even though you come from way over here and you live in Messina. You know what I mean. I talked to this lad the way we talk where I grew up, in the Albergheria in Palermo. So he would understand that we were Serious. We meant to Act.

I explained to him that we had been sent by the General himself, and that he was now the dictator of the island. His word was the new law. The General was The Big Man, now. [This phrase was written in Sicilian dialect, only later deciphered by Rob and me with the help of Sciascia.] And the General's new law says we are to eliminate those who have caused the problem, and so restore the law and Order of the Dictator to Castellnotte run rampant.

I explained to him that I knew he did not do this alone, if he did it at all. I understood that 'Comrade Tre' was covering up for someone. And while that might seem noble and loyal, what it meant, at bottom, was that he Gaetano was going to Die for whoever these others were. So then I offered the young man my opinion. "When you look at what they've done up there in that castle," I said to

192

the boy, "these other scoundrels you are protecting are not worth your loyalty, and certainly not your nobility."

So then I asked him straight out, "Who is Comrade Uno?"

But the lad was brave. He had a Big Heart, Rafaella. He answered without even a blink or a twitch, with just his courageous, foolish silence.

I told him that. Then I believed I understood something: it must be a woman the boy is so loyal to, I thought. "Or maybe, Gaetano, I should ask you this way: who is Comrade Una?"

This got somewhere, for he looked up in my eyes and I could see he wanted to spit at me then. But he was too smart. He said nothing, not a word, and he knew he'd already revealed too much.

"Okay," I said, "we'll have it your way, Comrade. Burtoni?" Together we pulled him up onto his feet and dragged the brave lad out into the church proper. "Bring them all up to the Castle," I ordered, and our men rounded up the twenty or so mute villagers and herded them like the sheep they were up to La Rocca. Burtoni and I led the boy Gaetano along at the head of them. The women and the old men of Castellnotte gradually gathered in a crowd following behind us. It was odd, but there were no children to be found, so I know that some of the women foresaw this trouble to come, and they hid their youngest away from it all.

We then dragged this lad Gaetano into that decimated orange garden and the people of the village followed us in. It is true, I was rough with the boy, I admit it, but you must be certain that I was hoping to get somewhere with them all. So while Sig. Burtoni held both our guns and our men held the twenty in a row so they would have to witness the execution, I tore the shirt off of his back and then I bound the boy's hands behind him, slowly and carefully, and tied a red bandanna around his eyes to blindfold him. All of this, I might add, Signorina, is more than what these cursed villagers did for the Duke and Duchess Burmonte. Then I shoved Gaetano down roughly on his knees so he knelt there bareback beside the burnt remains of the woodpile where the bodies of the duke and duchess lay.

"You and you and you," I picked out three men from among the villagers. "Take off your shirts, and spread them out like this." I took the boy Gaetano's white shirt and laid it like a blanket on the stones. When the three of them had done as I told them, I ordered them to cut the remains of the Duke and Duchess free and to spread their hideous corpses out onto those cloths before us, so that all could see them clearly. I'm afraid, O Signorina, that the joints in their hips and knees cracked and broke loose from their bodies when these men laid them out, and not one of the villagers who'd gathered to watch fell over fainting and sick, losing the contents of their stomachs, not even one of them, at that sound. Finally one of the now barebacked men collapsed on the stones, and the other two picked him up and helped him back to the row of the twenty.

"So this," I said, waving my arm down at the charred and now broken remains, and I was speaking in the plainest Sicilian I know, Signorina Rafaella, as close to the back and dark alleys of the Alberghia as I could. "This is what your friend young Gaetano here says that he has done, all alone. And for this, Under Orders from the Dictator General of the Kingdom of Sicily, we must execute him." I pulled the revolver out from my belt and pointed it straight at the boy's chest. "No one here knows anything more that might save this boy," I shouted, with my pistol pointed at the lad. "Just this one little boy did it all, set fire to the castle, cut down

194

these trees and burned this old man and this old woman alive here, all by himself."

There was a silence then that echoed loudly around the courtyard, and not even any birds sang, O Signorina. No one in the crowd even moved, much less spoke up in the poor lad's defense. So when I moved my thumb and cocked the hammer back on the pistol, it was loud and crisp in the still smoky air. "All you cowards are willing to let this one brave boy die for you. Or maybe Gaetano is the one and only wicked soul, and he deserves to die alone today."

Still there was nothing from any of them. I glanced over at Sig. Burtoni and he simply nodded his head once. But wait, my dearest Comrade Crisiana, I still had one more move to shake the infernal fruit loose from the tree, Rafaella.

"So be it," I said quietly. Then I announced in my most formal and northern Italian, "By order of the presiding General of the Island of Sicily, in the Kingdom of Italy, you, Gaetano of Castellnotte called 'Comrade Tre,' are sentenced hereby to death by gunfire." As I pulled the trigger, I noticed that your Sig. Burtoni, Rafaella, he closed his eyes. But you see, Signorina Crisiana, at the last moment I jerked the pistol to the side and fired into the ground, instead of into the boy's head. The poor lad collapsed in a faint onto the old stones anyway, and that was what did it, because it looked to all the world and to everyone in that garden as if he had been shot dead in an instant.

That was when, finally, a woman bolted out of the crowd screaming, "It wasn't him. It wasn't him." She ran out of the grasp of several of her neighbors who were trying to hold her back, and then she threw herself beside the boy, lifting up his head. At her touch, Gaetano came around with a start, terrified and confused, blindfolded and bound still, he struggled in the woman's hands and fell over onto his other side. But she was saying his name, cooing at him, and she pulled the blindfold from his eyes, so that his eyes snapped all around, wide and frightened. Slowly she, and then he, realized that he hadn't been shot.

Sig. Burtoni said to her, "Simone?" She was, apparently, another of the servants who waited upon the Duchess in that castle. Someone I believe that you, Rafaella, know well from your time in Castellnotte. Burtoni was truly distressed, Signorina, because he too knew these people, and because he knew very well these were old friends of yours. He knew what this all meant to you, although he could hardly realize what was about to happen to him; O dearest Rafaella, a very earthquake in his soul was bearing down on him. Bearing down like a wraith. And he could not know it was coming. None of us could know.

"Who was it?" I spoke to this Simone. She was, truly, a handsome woman with wild raven hair and dark, deep eyes, someone the men of this village all loved, I am sure. But Burtoni tells me, and I'm certain he has understood this from you, Signorina Crisiana, Simone was someone who was often pursued by young men, but had refused all their proposals. She was someone who dreamed of leaving Castellnotte, of life in Palermo of Napoli, or even in Rome. And her beauty was such that it might have carried her that far, given even part of an opportunity.

"If it wasn't him, Signorina," I said to her, "then tell me, who was it?" But she just ignored me, and doted on Gaetano, struggling to untie his hands. It went on like that for a time, and clearly they were once again refusing to talk, to respond, even to listen. Sig. Burtoni broke in and pulled Simone up onto her feet, and then, with some tears in his eyes (I must point these tears out to you, Rafaella) he bound her hands behind her and pulled Gaetano back up on his feet. But still they refused to answer us, and this lad

Gaetano spit on Sig. Burtoni when he was standing again. Burtoni just wiped the boy's spittle off his face, using it as a way to steal away his own tears. Yes, his tears, Rafaella, his Tears.

Still, the twenty stood in silence, and Gaetano with Simone beside him, was now insolent and defiant. I turned to the little crowd of townspeople, and said nothing at first, just pointed at the bodies of the Duke and Duchess, and then I said finally, "Will no one here speak the truth to us?"

The situation, Signorina Rafaella, was in danger of whirling out of our control. This defiance of the two of them, Gaetano and Simone, and the continued silence of the twenty, it could lead to another revolt if we let it continue. We already knew what these people were capable of doing. We might easily have a massacre on our hands. Not at all what Colonel Bixio commanded. Not order, but Pandemonium born of Anarchy.

"Blindfold them both," I ordered, but it was Burtoni who chose to do the work. He understood our orders, and he could see the situation arising. Once they were bound and blindfolded, he stepped alongside me, and drew his pistol out too. With a nod of his head, he let me see that all was ready.

I announced again, this time to both of them, the orders of Execution we served under. It was then that Sig. Burtoni and I together shot them, it was quick and I think painless, for they both lay dead and still on the stones in moments. They did not suffer, Rafaella. I can assure you of that. Our shots were true, and their pain was brief.

I believe I am reporting this all to you because of what happened next. This is why Burtoni asked me to write to you, Rafaella. As hard as it has been thus far on this path, it will be even harder still to report the rest of these dour events to you. But, O Signorina, I swear to you on all that is sacred to me, on my own freedom and on our Country and on my very heartbeat, what I write now (and indeed up to now) is the Certain and Definite Truth. These are the facts of what happened that day. They are not shaded or edited at all, they are the plain facts. I am sorry to report them as they are, but these are the true events of that day, without any addition or any omission.

It seems to me as I write this now that the pistol shots had not yet stopped echoing in our ears when I heard the commotion issuing from somewhere nearby. It was like the jabbering of dogs, and it came ringing up the hillside, cries and yells that were not intelligible even to me, they were I think so deeply in the tongue of Castellnotte. Perhaps they were not even words at all, just the random, ferocious sounds of anger and despair.

There were five of them, short and square to the ground, with wild gray hair curling out of scarves and their faces carved with wrinkles and sun, damp with the sweat of their anger. They carried long pointed sticks and poked and prodded at their man, and herded him toward us like a reluctant old cow. But it wasn't a cow, Signorina. All of us in the garden fell silent, with these now four dead bodies at our feet. But the five old women with their sticks in hand yapped and snarled, and the people of the village parted like sand on a creek bed to let them pass. They herded the man up to us, to Sig. Burtoni and me, and then the five old women pushed him onto the stones beside the still warm and bleeding bodies of Gaetano and Simone. This man was not bound or restrained in any way; he was instead surrounded by these snarling women, with their pointed sticks. He knelt there, afraid and trembling, dearest Rafaella, looking in shock at Simone and then at Gaetano, and not looking up at us.

But there was on Sig. Burtoni's face, you must know this too, O Signorina, a real horror now. We had all seen much on this day, too much to describe accurately, and enough to last us all the rest of our lives. But there was now a shock, a despair in Sig. Burtoni's eyes. His shoulders slumped down and the suffering man nearly dropped the revolver in his hand. He seemed more disturbed than the man kneeling on the ground beside Gaetano and Simone, before the ashes and bones of the Duke and Duchess.

Then two of the old women denounced their prisoner. While they spoke, the other three women continued with their cursing and snarling, and pounded their sticks on the stones. [Corrao now switches again into Sicilian, to report the words of these women. It was Sciascia again who translated the mysterious words for us.] "You have Killed the wrong ones," they said. "You have made a stupid mistake, because of these stupid men in our village. Here is the one they are protecting. We don't know why. You can have him. But kill no one else. Enough is enough. Take this one back to Messina where he came from. He doesn't belong to us anymore. Not after this. Not after what he has done here, out of hate."

I pointed down at the dead bodies of Gaetano and Simone. "Did these two have nothing to do with it?"

All five of the women spat out, not in any unison, but raggedly and one after another, "This is Comrade Uno."

I'm afraid, O Rafaella, that I have no need to tell you who this man was, the man they denounced. You know who it was, and you know what happened next, though you don't know how. You don't know how it happened that your father, Lombardo Crisiana, died.

I am sorry to have to tell you this, Signorina Rafaella, but he had been until then cowering like a lowly cur, driven by old women into our hands. He trembled and refused to look up, and he was nothing like the man who'd met us in the countryside near Messina. There was nothing in him of the courage and determination of Sole who started us out on our patrol with Rosalino Pilo, and with you, O Rafaella. He was broken and weak, and he had at that moment come apart.

I asked the crowd if this was all true, what the old women told us. It was only then that the twenty began to speak, and everything spilled out: the way Lombardo had promised them all their own piece of the land, promised everyone would be free and independent of their debts, and Castellnotte would truly belong to them, to the people who worked the ground, if only they would seize the castle from the Duke. I don't need to tell you this. You know it, in your heart. You know, Rafaella, what he believed and what it led him to do. The twenty spilled it all out then. But what you can't imagine was how weak and ashamed your father seemed, as the people of his home Castellnotte turned on him, and as those old women continued to prod and poke at him with their pointed sticks like he was a cornered, rabid dog.

Again Pandemonium was on the verge of sweeping over us, and the whole crowd was close to losing all Control. I could see this, they were beginning to close in on him like he was a wounded predator. I knew again I had to stop it all at once, before it even started. So I pronounced the sentence on him, almost word for word as it was for Gaetano and Simone. Hearing those words announced—the Order of Execution—seemed to bring a strange calm and courage back to Lombardo.

The old women sensed this change and stopped, and he climbed back up onto his feet. Suddenly he was the Sole we all knew from the beginning days of this revolt. He lifted his head, and shook it so his silver hair fell about his shoulders. And then Sole spoke to the townspeople. "You know, though you turn on me now, you know the truth of what we have done. It was my grandfather who planted these hillsides with grapes and olives. It was he, with the help of your parents and grandparents, who restored those fields until they were full and rich. He passed their fruit down to all of us, and not to a couple of old barren aristocrats, foreign to this land, not even Sicilians. It was he who laid the stones we stand on in this garden. These trees we have cut down and burned, he planted them for us. They were planted for us, for all of us, but in the end they didn't belong to any of us. They were locked away so you could only see them if you worked here. Worked for them.

"All this wealth and all the fruits of our work belonged to only them," Sole didn't need to indicate in anyway the charred bodies lying on the torn cloth before him. "They took it all, because they were born to it, you know. It was given to them by their blood, these two people, who could barely even talk to us. They could barely speak our language, and then only to give us orders. It was all theirs. The fruit of my grandfather's and my father's and of my labor. It was all theirs. And we, We who Worked this ground, Worked these hills, we received only what they handed down to us. Scraps from their grand tables, where our children served them. It was these children here who waited on them," and Sole turned and gazed down at the still remains of Gaetano and Simone.

"O, certainly, they were generous in handing out the fruits of the land to all of us, helping us when we were sick or in trouble. They were kind and gentle, even. And me, they helped to send me off to school while my family, my wife and daughter, worked in their great house. They were kind and forgiving, and they stooped down to help us up.

"But I tell you all, every one of you, none of this was theirs to give. None of it." Sole stopped there, and the people were quiet for a moment longer. "I guess it was not their fault." He went on. "Perhaps we should have returned their kindness, but it was not in my heart to save the old masters. And," the man we called Sole gazed defiantly around at the crowd of villagers. "And it was not in you, either, to forgive them their tiny, brutal arrogance. The arrogance of the entitled, or of those who feel entitled only because of who you are."

It was our Sig. Burtoni then, O dearest Rafaella, who interrupted his speech. Sig. Burtoni burst in, with a long angry moan that sounded so tortured it surprised even me. "I knew them, Lombardo," he bellowed out, and your father, Rafaella, he stopped and turned to look at him. There was hatred then in your father's eyes, O Signorina, and as I write this now, I don't understand it. We were all comrades in arms, together, after all. We all fought side by side across Sicilia, to free her. But the hatred in Lombardo's eyes made him—I'm sorry to write this, O Signorina—it made him seem small again. He shrank in my eyes, in all our eyes, at that moment.

Sig. Burtoni went on, in almost a whisper then, and every one of us, the twenty, the villagers, the old women, the red shirts and I, and even Lombardo, we all leaned forward to hear his soft words. "They are not as you say, Sole," he called your father by his old rebel name. "I knew the Duke and the Duchess too, if only briefly. She was hard and proud, but the Duke had a heart as true as this Sicilian sun in spring. And the Duchess, she liked to give orders, but who among us doesn't know a woman with a big heart, a mamma, a nonna, a zia vecchia who likes to give orders. It only means that she cares. We know this, it only means she is worried for us.

"They did not deserve to die this way, Lombardo, and at your hands. If we dream of this island as part of a great country, we cannot go this way, Lombardo, with old hatreds. The old hatreds have to die, along with our old ways. The Counts and Countesses, the Dukes and Duchesses, even the Kings and Queens, they have to be part of us. This is why the General has sent us here," and then Burtoni changed and began to address him with that old red shirt name we knew him by first. "Sole, these are the Orders of the General himself. He is now the Dictator, Sole, the very Law of this Land. Until we all bury these old hatreds, Sole, only then can we be Free."

I hesitate again to tell you this all, Signorina Crisiana. But I fear you must know the whole of it, if I am to do my service to Burtoni, and indeed to you, dear Rafaella. I am sorry to go on, but go on to the end we must.

Rafaella, your father swore then at Burtoni so fiercely he literally spat out these words. "My hatred of them will never be buried, not even in their burned and abandoned graves."

"Then this is the order of the General, Sole, and we must fulfill it," Sig. Burtoni said as he raised his pistol to aim it at Lombardo Crisiana, known in the movement as Sole, your father.

But Burtoni did not execute the order, Signorina. And anyone who was there will attest to this. Jack Burton did not execute your father, O Rafaella, even though he raised a gun to his head, and even though he surely intended to follow his orders. He did not do it, Rafaella. Burtoni did not do it.

It is a hard thing to write this to you, and I suspect you will not believe me. You are likely to think that I am only trying to hide from you what our friend Burtoni did. But Rafaella, O Signorina, that is not true.

This, my dearest Rafaella, is the Truth.

I shot your father. It did it quickly, to spare Burtoni this deed, because I knew well from all our days together, yours Rafaella and mine and his, I knew how he loved you, and how it would burden him to do the task we had been ordered to do.

So I shot Lombardo Crisiana. I will tell you only that he died quickly, if not well.

I report these facts to you fully, Signorina Crisiana. It was I, known to you as Giovanni Corrao, who Executed the

Orders of Colonel Nino Bixio on that day, 2 September 1860, in the gardens of Castellnotte, in the newly Free Kingdom of Sicilia. Long Live Italia!

I report this final truth to you, as well. Though our comrade Mr. Jack Burton, who is called by us Gianni Burtoni, though he was present and participated in the police proceedings of that time, he did not Execute Sig. Lombardo Crisiana, your father, our comrade in arms, known by the name of Sole to the Thousand who marched with the General.

I swear to this on the truth of the Thousand Red Shirts, and on all that they have won for Italia.

Signed,

Giovanni Corrao, son of the Albergheria

Post Script: You have, Signorina, I understand, visited their graves. I feel I must also report to you that it was not Burtoni or I who chose the place. It was the people of Castellnotte who buried them high on the mountainside above La Rocca, and it was the People of Castellnotte who insisted that they all, the five of them, be buried together side by side, in order to remember the Tragedy of the whole event.

This ends the complete text, which Rob and I found within that plain manila envelope.

The following morning Lombardo Sciascia took us up the hill to visit the castle grounds, and despite what he'd said the day before, he led us inside into the orange garden.

There were young trees, with blood red oranges on them, growing in pots where the stones had carefully been replaced and cleaned. Above us we could hear the sounds of power tools and men talking, as they worked to restore the Castle to its old glory. Lombardo Sciascia took us over to the very central tree and pointed down to a carved stone plaque with the date and a series of names on it, laid carefully in the stone floor of the garden. It bore that date "2 SEPTEMBRE 1860" on it, and then it read simply, in Italian, "In this garden these heroes lost their lives for the Risorgimento: Gaetano Boldoni – age 17 years; Simone Martelli- age 19 years; William and Elizabeth Shawcross, the Duke and Duchess of Burmonte – ages unknown; Lombardo Crisiana – age 64 years."

"I think this is what Sister Teresa wanted you to see," Sciascia told us. "And I think she wanted you to read that letter, the way Jack Burton didn't." He spoke Burton's name in straight flat English. There was no 'Burtoni' to it, so it sounded out roughly amongst all the Italian.

"Burton?" I said.

"He was here? You met him?" Rob added a little too quickly.

Sciascia laughed and nodded his head. "How do you think he found my sister in Siracusa?"

Rob and I were lost then. Jack Burton's journey was the reverse of ours, it seemed. He must have started out by coming back here, to Castellnotte, where these executions occurred, where surely his love affair with Rafaella Crisiana ended.

Lombardo Sciascia went on to describe the old man. "A couple of years ago, he arrived here on the bus like you two, in his wheelchair, of course. But he was so strong in the arms he almost didn't need help getting out of the bus. It dropped him here in the Piazza San Lucia, just like it did you two. Right away he started to work his way up to La Rocca here in that wheelchair, all on his own, and so some of us started to help him along. It was Cinzia and Lara, I think.

"At any rate, when they realized where he was going, Lara came running to get me. But I was gone to Grammiche to visit friends, just like I was yesterday. So it wasn't until I got off the late bus, and Cinzia sent her two boys Enrico and Andrea to meet me. 'Come down to La Scala,' they said, and took me by the hand, almost dragging me along.

"There at the top of the stairs, where I took you boys yesterday, right there sat this Jack Burton, in his wheel chair. It was the first time I saw him. And Big Andrea, Cinzia's husband, was sitting next to him and they were drinking wine, and Jack Burton was gazing out at the sea, and down at the stairs. He was talking away, spinning yarns about the days of the Thousand, as if he'd been there himself. That's what Andrea told me later.

"So the two lads led me out there, and they explained who I am, you see. That's when old Burton, with his icy blue eyes in that deep rutted brow, his eyes seemed to go blind. He's looking out at the sea, still, but he seemed blind now, from something he sees inside himself. And he wouldn't believe me, at first, you know."

"Wait a minute, Signor Lombardo," Rob said. "What are you talking about?"

Sciascia looked at us as if we were idiots. "I thought that was why Sister Teresa sent you here. You are connected with this Burton fellow, somehow. True?"

"We are," I said.

Rob was quicker that me, he had begun to catch on. "Signor Sciascia, who are you?"

"I thought you lads knew. Why, what the devil is up now." Sciascia threw both hands up in the air with real exasperation, and he muttered to himself, "What the hell are you up to now, Rafaella?"

The sound of that name on his lips pulled us both up short. "Who are you?" I said, quietly, looking down at the plaque full of names written in stone. A ripe blood orange had fallen there beside it, waiting obviously for one of us to pick it up.

"Who are you, Signore?" Rob repeated.

He pointed at the names on the plaque, and then he said, "Lombardo Crisiana was my great-grandfather."

There was silence for a moment as both Rob and I began to piece it together. "My sister Rafaella, though she denies it now by changing her name, she was named after our grandmother."

"And your grandmother is . . .?" Rob said, his eyes as wide as mine.

"Our grandmother was Rafaella Crisiana. That letter from Corrado was addressed to her. This is how I have come to possess it. And it is how my sister Rafaella came to have this journal that she gave to you young lads, I haven't seen that journal for a lot of years, since I was just a boy."

I glanced over to Rob. "That means Sister Teresa at the Domus Mariae is . . . "

"Yes, my sister Rafaella Sciascia."

"But?" I said, still trying to sort it all out.

"And my sister has stolen my dear, my only daughter and lured her off to the convent. My little Rosalina."

Rob began to nod his head up and down slowly. "And your daughter Rosalina, she is named after . . .?"

"She bears our mother's name, Rosalina Sciascia, that is except for now she is a damned nun, Sister Chiara. Because my sister lured her away from us."

Then Lombardo Sciascia stopped, looked at that orange on the ground, and crossed himself, muttering a prayer of forgiveness.

"I got it," Rob said. Then he helped me out. "Rafaella Crisiana had a baby daughter, right Signor Sciascia? And she was named Rosalina."

As Lombardo Sciascia nodded in silent agreement, Rob just looked at me, and said, "Pilo."

"I don't believe it," I said.

"This is just exactly what that Jack Burton said, until I showed him Corrado's letter," said Sciascia.

"And then you told Burton about your daughter in Siracusa, just like you told us, didn't you?" Rob said.

"That's right."

"And that was how Burton found his way to Domus Mariae." Rob pressed on, linking the fragments together that even Lombardo Sciascia hadn't understood.

"Yes, in a damned all to hell hurry, too, with barely a thank you to me," Sciascia said.

"Pilo," I repeated.

The ride back to Siracusa seemed shorter, though it still took all the rest of that day. A large part of it was traveled in silence, though we did see the schoolchildren climb on and ride with us a while, getting off again, going home, to all their little villages along the way. The two girls tried out their English again, a little braver now, quicker to speak. The bus was quieter in general, because it was not market day the way it was the day before, and also because it was the end of the school day. We were all tired.

For most of the ride I just leafed through Burton's old journal, reading around in it randomly. At one point, as the

AST maneuvered to turn around in some tiny piazza, I said to Rob, "So it's Rosalino Pilo, isn't it? He is the grandfather of our old Sister Teresa, who was born Rafaella like her grandmother." Rob didn't answer, he just listened. "And Pilo, then, is the great-grandfather of the little sorella, Sister Chiara. That is why her real name is Rosalina. After Pilo, am I right?"

Rob nodded thoughtfully, but he still didn't answer. Something about it all seemed wrong, and it wouldn't go away. And we both sensed it.

It was turning dark by the time the bus returned across Ponte Umbertino. And then Rob said out loud, not expecting any answer, "But why did the old Sister send us off to Castellnotte? I don't understand."

We arrived at Domus Mariae hoping there might be a room, only to find Sister Chiara at the desk, waiting for us, holding our room open without a reservation.

"How did you know we'd be back?" I said.

"I didn't," she answered. "I'm just doing what Sister Teresa told me to do."

So then the little Sister led us upstairs, and warned us not to bump our heads again, and threw open the balcony windows to let in the moonlit sea air, just as she did on my first night there. And she welcomed us back, handing me the key, and to Rob she handed another plump manila envelope, addressed this time to both our names. "How is my father?" she asked. But we had trouble answering, as we stared at that fat package in Rob's hands.

Finally he said, though still distracted, " He misses you. Your father, Rosalina, if I may use that name, he misses you."

She said nothing more, except, " Chiara is my name now, Signori."

Once the little Sister was gone, and while we were still standing in the middle of the room beside our bags, Rob tore open the envelope. From inside it he pulled out a letter, written by the old Sister. There was a small gray key taped to the top of the first page. "Why didn't she give us this before we left for Castellnotte?" Rob asked me, not expecting any answers. "Why did she send us there?"

Then he started to read her letter, and I took the manila envelope out of his hand. Inside it I found what Rob, in his haste, hadn't noticed yet.

"Well, I'll be damned," he whispered, as he was reading.

From out of the envelope I pulled four loose pages written in a hand I recognized well, a hand I'd just spent a bit of time with lately. They were the missing four pages from Jack Burton's journal, the pages cut out so carefully. And now, as you'll see when you read them, we know that it was Burton himself who removed them. He was the one who cut them out so carefully hoping they wouldn't be missed, when Rafaella Crisiana read this history. He believed those pages would never be missed, but once the binding of the journal had broken and fallen apart with age, it revealed the two little slips of cut paper still sewn into the book, where they had been carefully sliced out.

This is what I found that Burton wrote there:

I don't know now what to do. Somehow he has found me out, probably from the damned slips of my own stupid tongue. I spoke too much, O I shot off my mouth, I went on about meeting the General in Montevideo, and about the Anzani Brigade in '48, about dear old Francesco Anzani himself. This must be how he figured it out, from out of my own braggart's mouth.

And I should have known too, the way he interrogated me. He wanted details, the kind of little details like the names of horses and the height of my Ciccio Anzani and the color of his hair, and even the names of the streets and piazzas in Morazzone. And proudly, stupidly, damnably, I answered them all. As effortlessly as if I'd been there, because of course, I was there. Damn my own flapping, open chattering mouth. What was I thinking?

It was clear he didn't believe me at first. He thought I was lying, you see. And he thought that because he was smart enough to realize I had to be lying, I couldn't have been there; it all happened over ten years ago. Fifteen if you're counting from the days in Argentina, though I really don't go back that far with the General in South America. For most of those years I was on my own in the wanderer's world. So Lombardo thought he had me. He thought I had to be lying, because a boy as young as I am now would have been just a little child, way back then, ten years before.

But no, I couldn't shut myself up. I let my stupid pride overcome my common sense. I suppose I was showing off for him, bragging about my days at sea and in the saddle alongside the great General himself, because after all I was about to ask permission to marry his daughter. I was just working up my courage to ask. And I wanted to seem big and important to him, this little rebel leader from Messina, raised in pretty little Castellnotte by his peasant father. I wanted, standing there in front of him, to be a big man, before I asked for his daughter's hand. So I told him the story of how I got my name from il Generalissimo. O Rafaella.

But old Sole is one sharp individual. He added up the years, once I'd passed this test. When he quietly came to believe that I wasn't lying to him, that I was indeed telling him the truth, then he knew something horrible was wrong with me. I wasn't human, at least not in his eyes.

So being Sole, he confronted me. No messing around for him. He just asked me straight out, "How old are you?"

I wanted to marry his daughter. But Rafaella, I haven't even told her yet about my cursed affliction. She doesn't know my age either. I am still afraid to tell her the truth, because it may frighten her. She might flee, if she understood what I am, for I am a monster. And it all leaves me so alone, so perpetually alone.

But I could not lie to Lombardo. Not anymore. It would not have mattered, even if I had tried to lie to him. He knows something is not right with me. So, I just told him the truth, as far as I know it. What else could I do? It was too late for me to lie to him anymore.

He sat for a long while digesting what I told him, and then asked me feebly a few questions I couldn't answer. "How?" he said. And even worse, "Why?"

I told him, "I wish I knew."

Then suddenly the worst that I can imagine happened. He rose up on his feet from the table where we were sitting over a pitcher of red wine. He said, "I have seen the way my little Rafaella looks at you. And I have seen the way you return her gaze. I am telling you this now, so that it won't become a problem. Stay away from her." He began pointing at me with his finger, in his violent, bossy way. "If I see you even speaking to her, even in the same room with her, I swear to you now, and have not a moment's doubt that I mean this: If I ever even hear your name spoken in her presence, I will come looking for you, and I will slit your monstrous throat myself. And if I can't slit it, someone in my family will do it for me. Do you understand? It will do you no good to get rid of me. If I am gone, the family will take care of it.

"Do you understand?"

I came asking for her hand. But in a moment of foolish pride, I have lost her forever.

Lombardo is right, of course. I am a monster. I have no right to ruin her life. It is as it should be.

Alone. Always.

*   *   *

There, about half way down the page, the writing stopped abruptly. I gazed for a while at the handwriting, pondering what it meant. Then slowly I understood, I think, why Jack Burton had so carefully sliced these few pages out of his journal. It wasn't just to hide his insane secret, for there are plenty of hints all through this notebook surrounding his strange and impossible age. It wasn't just to hide that. He was giving this journal to Rafaella, to win back her heart. It is why he had Giovanni Corrao write the letter to her, urging Corrao to take the blame for her father's death. And really, what difference did it make to Corrao, our slippery Dottore Calogero, who got blamed for an ordered execution. Something about his letter didn't ring all that true. So there it was, in the end, the only reason for Burton to carefully remove these very few pages, before he sent them into the hands of his one, true love.

"You've got to read this," Rob interrupted my thoughts, holding out the letter toward me. "You won't believe this," she said. "I think she's crazy."

I didn't reply, I just handed Rob the four journal pages. He knew, just as I had, what they were. But he didn't know yet what was in them.

"Here is Jack Burton's motive," I said, then I paused and swallowed hard. "There were not just orders to execute Lombardo Crisiana. There was a motive to murder him, too. There's a reason Jack Burton had to see Lombardo Crisiana dead and gone." Rob's eyes seemed to darken at that, but he couldn't object. He just took the papers from my hands.

The new letter was from Sister Teresa, in her neat and careful hand. She wrote to us in a very simple Italian too, I could tell because I could read it all so easily. It was undated, and it bore just our first names at the top, next to the little flat key she'd gently secured with cellophane tape. It read:

These are the missing pages from the journal of Gianni Burtoni, which I gave you to read earlier. You'll see, if you try, that they fit perfectly inside the notebook. The journal, along with the letter my brother showed you, were sent by mail to our grandmother, Rafaella Crisiana, who rode with the Thousand in 1859. These missing pages, she told me, arrived some days later, delivered at night by hand by a masked stranger on horseback from Palermo, who would not use nor leave any name, though he spoke only in Sicilian, and did not seem to understand Italian.

Please do not show even one line of this to young Sister Chiara. And please do not speak to her of these matters. She does not know who she is. And she must not know. Only I know, and now you too. And of course, Burtoni knows as well.

Once you have read them, please return all of these papers to this envelope, and leave them in the top drawer of the desk in this room. The key at the top of this page will lock the drawer and keep all of this safe and secure from curious eyes until I return. Once you have locked this all up, please throw the key away into the sea. I have the only other.

You know now what I am doing. My brother and I are the grandchildren of Jack Burton. [Sister Teresa here, and at several other key places in this letter, reverts to calling Burton by his English name. I am not sure why, but the name always seems to appear at a crucial point when the old nun needs perhaps to distance herself from the evil she calls by that English name.] Our mother, Rosalina Crisiana Sciascia died at a very advanced age, in a violent crash of an automobile, in 1922. However, she always seemed youthful for her age, and everyone remarked on it constantly. My brother and I were raised by our father alone, Gaetano Sciascia, who died some years ago. He of course did not suffer the curse.

Because of the grace and wisdom of God, I entered the convent as a young girl, and so I have never had any children. My brother's wife died young, may God rest Rosetta's soul, and my brother Lombardo has not remarried. You understand, this means that my niece Rosalina Sciascia, you know her as Sister Chiara, she is the last of the line of Jack Burton and Rafaella Crisiana.

It is perhaps too early to tell. I don't know if my brother or I have inherited the curse of Burtoni's blood. We seem, at least to my eyes, to be growing old happily and well, as we should. And my brother suspects nothing. I only came to understand Signor Burtoni's curse when I read over these pages myself, the same one's you have read. And I did not believe them at first. I did not believe a word of this raving until Signor Burtoni appeared on the doorstep of Domus Mariae, asking questions about me and about Sister Chiara. He did not know who I was, and I did not tell him my name. With time, he went away.

I repeat. Sister Chiara knows nothing of any of this. It must remain so, to praise heaven that protects us.

My brother probably complained to you in Castellnotte of the way I "stole" his daughter. I know that he misses her, as she looks so much like her mother, his wife. I know he complained of his loneliness there, without his wife or his only child. But he has never understood what we are involved in. The abomination. It was only the grace of Our Lord and his Holy Mother that led Sister Chiara to me. I prayed long and hard on it, and I have at last come to see that this is the will of God.

Great longevity in life is not a blessing. Though it is often confused for luck, it is not. Only the weak and mistaken dream in their fragile souls of cheating Death, that is all it is. I pray each day, now that Sister Chiara is safe and taken care of in the Order, that if indeed my brother and I have inherited the curse within this bloodline, I pray that we may suffer a sudden and easy death, just as our mother did. I know it is a strange thing to pray for your own death to come soon. But I do. And I pray also that my dear niece, Sister Chiara, will find her end easily, and most importantly, in a goodly time.

*   *   *

I have kept this secret from everyone, even from my family. When Burton appeared here, well, you understand the danger his very existence creates. He is a monster of God, some left over fragment of an Old Testament disorder, unleashed mistakenly on our world.

This is why I have told you these truths here. When you arrived at Domus Mariae looking for him, asking for Jack Burton, describing him, I realized that you two have been sent for him. It is not enough here in Ortigia that I hide these truths from a foolish and depraved world, and that I bring this monstrous line of blood to an end here. You have been sent to me for a reason. Providence is taking care of this curse, in its own way, beyond our understanding. The Lord is providing a way.

Perhaps you have been sent here as angels of Death, to bring this horrible creature to his end. So leave you this information: One year ago we received a letter here at Domus Mariae from him, addressed to Sister Chiara and to me. Fortunately, I saw it before my niece did. I burned it, unopened, destroyed it with fire. Where his soul will end, I believe. His letter is gone, and I know not what was inside it.

May God be with you, in your pursuit of Jack Burton. May you release him at last from his hell. I know only this. The letter came from Jesi.

God bless you in your journey.

Sorella Teresa, once Rafaella Sciascia

At the bottom of the last page she wrote: "Never return here," in English so it could not be misunderstood.

"Does she really think we're out to kill him?" Rob said to me, the moment my eyes rose from the page.

"She's nuts," I repeated.

"And where the hell is Jesi?" Rob said, immediately.

"Oh no. Oh no you don't, Rob. My time is up. I've got classes and students back in the Midwest waiting for me, and a plane ticket out of Catania day after tomorrow. I've got to get back to my life. Enough of God damned Jack Burton."

But Rob was looking past me out the window at the sea. "God damned Jack Burton," he said. Then I swear I heard him mutter under his breath, "Jesi."

The next morning I locked up all the papers in the desk drawer, just the way the Old Nun in her madness wanted them. I was going to toss the key out of the window into the sea just as she wanted, but Rob took it from me, and pocketed it. It's clear he isn't done with old Jack Burton just yet.

In the early afternoon, little Sister Chiara was back at the desk, with her big brown eyes and her smooth olive skin and those slightly plump lips, and I told her I would be checking out in the morning. Her brown eyes seemed disappointed genuinely, and I thought for a moment I would change my mind and stay. But then it occurred to me, somehow, to ask her how old she was. She seemed so very young. I actually opened my mouth to speak, before I told myself to be silent. Perhaps I didn't really want to know that answer.

"Where is Jesi?" Rob asked her, and again she didn't seem surprised.

In fact, she reached down in a fold that hid a pocket in her habit, and pulled out a little map of Italy with a circle on it around the city of Jesi, and she handed it over to Rob. "Jesi is near Ancona," she said. "In Le Marche."

The little Sister was so pretty I wanted to say, let's go there together. But that was just an urge. I have responsibilities, so I didn't speak.

Rob took the map, and said, "Sister Teresa," matter-of-factly.

Sister Chiara nodded her pretty head and smiled yes. Then she pulled out another slip of paper from that same hidden pocket, folded over with my brother's full name written on it. "You have a phone message, too. Someone called early this morning for you, asking for 'Mister Robert,' and they said it was important. It was the company, MacLendon Petrolio, he said. They need to hear from you as soon as possible. But Sister Teresa told me not to disturb your room until both of you gentlemen were finished and checked out of it completely." She pronounced our last name, and the name of the oil company awkwardly, with those pretty plump lips, and again I daydreamed of slipping away with her.

There was just a phone number on that slip of paper. Rob looked worried, and disappointed too, because that number was familiar. You see, his time was up too. "So much for my trip to Jesi," he frowned as he eyed the number.

And he was right. The company wanted him in the Gulf of Mexico, and soon. So he was on a flight from Rome to Dallas, just six or seven hours behind mine. Everyday life was calling him back, too, and so much for Sister Teresa's Angels of Death. So much for Jack Burton, who'd once again given us the slip.

But Rob did leave for Texas behind me by at least half a day. Which gave him plenty of time, a whole morning I'd say, to make some copies before he threw that tiny key away into the deep blue Ionian Sea.

ALSO BY SANDRO DARIOSTO

THE LAST GOOD RUN

BURTON THE RED:
An omnibus edition containing the first three adventures of
Jack Burton, including

IN THE NORTH

BEYOND ASPROMONTE

Forthcoming from per sempre Anita Edizione:

HANDS OF THE BIRD AND OTHER STORIES

THE WISDOM RUN